Praise for Dream on, Amber

"Funny, poignant...[a] wise and accessible read for nine- to twelve-year-olds."

—*The Wall Street Journal*

"Emma Shevah's *Dream on, Amber* is narrated in a spunky, endearing voice by Amber Miyamoto... Though *Dream on, Amber* is ripe with opportunities for didacticism, Amber's appealingly oddball voice makes the lessons go down easy."

—*The New York Times*

★ "[This] novel is a charmer... While its humor and illustrations lend it Wimpy Kid appeal, its emotional depth makes it stand out from the pack. *Molto bene!*"

—*Booklist*, Starred Review

★ "Shevah tenderly captures the void of growing up without a father yet manages to create a feisty, funny heroine. A gutsy girl in a laugh-out-loud book that navigates tough issues with finesse."

—*Kirkus Reviews*, Starred Review

★ "Amber's effervescent and opinionated narration captivates from the start, making it easy to root for her as she strives to conquer the 'beast' of her worries and thrive at home and at school."

—*Publishers Weekly*, Starred Review

★ "Shevah breathes life into this middle schooler, her lively family members, and her classmates and teachers. By turns playful and poignant, in both style and substance, this coming-of-age novel will hook readers from the first page to the last."

—*School Library Journal*, Starred Review

"Amber makes an approachable and admirable guide through questions of identity encountered by many tween readers...the final product, with its message of love, self-acceptance, and forgiveness is like one of those cakes with beets snuck in: sweet, tasty, and surprisingly nourishing."

—*Bulletin of the Center for Children's Books*

PRAISE FOR *DARA PALMER'S MAJOR DRAMA*

★ "Following *Dream on, Amber* (2015), Shevah returns with another book, this time deftly navigating the complexity of being a transracial adoptee...this funny, charismatic heroine will capture her readers' hearts."

—*Kirkus Reviews*, Starred Review

Emma Shevah

sourcebooks
jabberwocky

Sourcebooks and the colophon are registered trademarks of Sourcebooks, Inc.

Published by Sourcebooks Jabberwocky,
an imprint of Sourcebooks, Inc.
P.O. Box 4410, Naperville, Illinois 60567-4410
(630) 961-3900
Fax: (630) 961-2168
www.sourcebooks.com

Originally published as Dream on, Amber in 2014 in Great Britain by The Chicken House.

Library of Congress Cataloging-in-Publication data is on file with the publisher.

Source of Production: LSC Communications, Crawfordsville, IN, USA
Date of Production: September 2019
Run Number: POD

Printed and bound in the United States of America.
POD 10 9 8 7 6 5 4 3 2

This book is dedicated to
children all over the world
who—for one reason or another—
are growing up without a father.
I know how it feels.
This book is for you.

One-Uno-Ichi

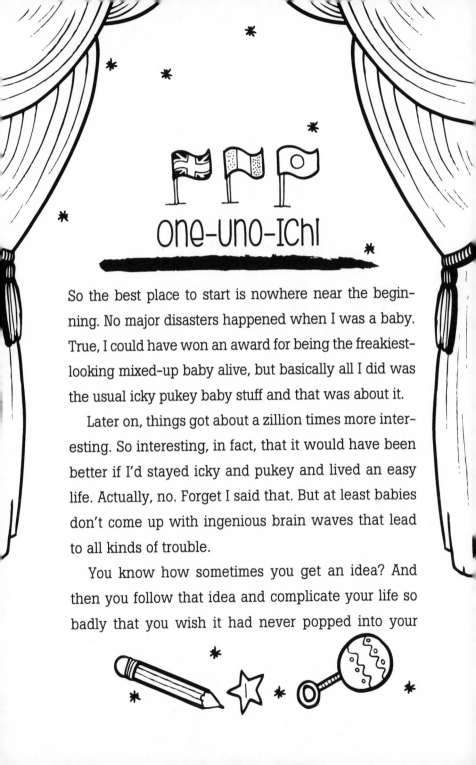

So the best place to start is nowhere near the beginning. No major disasters happened when I was a baby. True, I could have won an award for being the freakiest-looking mixed-up baby alive, but basically all I did was the usual icky pukey baby stuff and that was about it.

Later on, things got about a zillion times more interesting. So interesting, in fact, that it would have been better if I'd stayed icky and pukey and lived an easy life. Actually, no. Forget I said that. But at least babies don't come up with ingenious brain waves that lead to all kinds of trouble.

You know how sometimes you get an idea? And then you follow that idea and complicate your life so badly that you wish it had never popped into your head? Yeah. That's what happened. Me and my genius ideas.

It's not all bad though. Something good came of it. Something amazing, actually. Something that changed my life.

But before I tell you about my idea, there are some things about me you should know or you just won't get what I'm talking about. So here goes.

My name is

AMBRA ALESSANDRA LEOLA KIMIKO MIYAMOTO.

I have no idea why my parents gave me all those hideous names but they must have wanted to ruin my life, and you know what? They did an amazing job. Obviously I don't use them all because it would take me about a month just to tell people what I'm called. Officially, my name is Ambra, which sounds fine in an Italian accent because the "m" sounds like you're chewing a toffee and you've got that roly-poly "r." But not when English people say it because they say *Am bra*. I am a bra. This is beyond embarrassing because I don't even need one yet.

So I use the English version of my name, which is AMBER.

I have this crazy name because I'm half Italian and half Japanese. It's not easy to be half this and half that, especially two halves that are so completely different. I'm nearly twelve, and I live in South London with my mum and my little sister, Bella. My dad doesn't live with us. He was a Japanese computer science student and he met my mum at Kingston University. That's where the last name Miyamoto comes from (Japan, not Kingston University). But we don't see him anymore. Which is kind of what triggered this whole business.

But before I get to the messy stuff, you need to know more about my family or this just won't make any sense. It might not make any sense anyway, but at least you'll get the whole picture.

So for starters, my mum's name is Bob, and she's a graphic designer. Having a mother called Bob might

BELLA

MUM

3

seem embarrassing (and trust me, it is) but her full name is Roberta Fiorella Santececca Miyamoto, so Bob is actually an improvement.

Her hair is wild and curly, and she dyes it all shades from red to purple. She wears bright glittery dresses, big biker boots, and dangly earrings, and that's for Sunday afternoon shopping trips—you should see her when she's going out in the evening. And she has this colorful tattoo of a koi on her lower back. Koi is the Japanese name for a carp, but a carp sounds like a stupid thing to tattoo on your skin, and a koi sounds romantic and interesting. I think the tattoo was for my dad. Mum says it "symbolizes strength and determination" but I think it means something cheesy like "I love your fishy face" or "your soul is forever hooked to mine" or something.

My genius idea didn't have that much do with my mum. But it had everything to do with BeLLA.

She's six and she got lucky: my parents must have used up their entire list of hideous names on me because she's just Isabella, and they even shortened that. She was born in a Mini Cooper on the way to the hospital because she came out way too fast. My dad had to zip into a supermarket parking lot on the way to St George's and deliver her on the backseat, which is totally gross because we still own that car and I have to sit in it. I refuse to sit in the back though, unless Nonna (my grandma) is coming with us and then I have no choice. But Bella loves it and invites all her friends and teachers to come and see where she started out in the world. And now on every car trip, she counts the other Mini Coopers on the road and thinks that's how many babies have been born since we left the house. So, unlike me, she came out in a weird way and has carried on being weird ever since.

Bella's seriously obsessed with pink, but don't think she's some cute fairy princess because she isn't. She's super bossy and *molto* embarrassing. (*Molto* is the

Italian word for "very"—these words just pop out from time to time.) She likes playing dress-up when we go out, even to the shop up the road, and always asks a zillion random questions. She makes me take her to the park to feed the ducks and tells them stories in a really loud voice so you wish you'd never agreed to take her. And when she's going to sleep, she picks her nose and wipes it on the wall, which means she has boogers stuck right next to her head. That is right up there with the top ten most disgusting things I have ever seen.

I'm warning you: the heartbreaking part is coming up so if you don't like sad stuff you can go off and watch TV or something.

If you're still reading, this is what happened.

When I was six years old and Bella was one, my dad left home and never came back. I don't know why. Maybe Mum and Dad had a big fat argument. Maybe they had lots of them; I don't remember. And that was the end of that.

I have no idea where my dad is now. I don't even know if he's alive or dead because he never writes and he never calls. He doesn't turn up to see our school

plays or take us to the zoo on Sundays like other dads who have left home. He doesn't send us birthday cards even though he obviously knows when our birthdays are because he was there when we were born. He just left one night without saying good-bye and I haven't seen him since.

Mum doesn't like to talk about it. When I bring it up, she makes a face and says it's complicated and she'll explain when I'm older because until then, I just won't get it. It makes his departure kind of mysterious but in a bad way. Even if I don't get it, I'd still like to try because not knowing makes you imagine all kinds of things.

Maybe he spent all his time playing computer games so Mum strangled him and chucked his body in the River Thames.

Or the Japanese mafia kidnapped and tortured him for hacking into their secret website.

He might have got a big bonk on the head, lost his memory, and he's wandering around somewhere trying to remember who he is and where he lives.

He could have run off with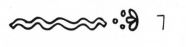

Miss Cronin, my first-grade teacher, because she left at about the same time. They say she went to another school but who knows?

Or maybe he was just cold and heartless and had no love to give so he went to live in a cave for the rest of his grumpy life and now he's a weird, twisted creature like Gollum in *The Hobbit.*

I'm sure the truth is far less exciting than all the things I imagine when I lie in bed.

I tried googling him once but I wasn't sure if any of the people who came up were really him. It kind of creeped me out, and then Mum walked into the room so I closed the page *veloce.* It felt so icky and weird to do an Internet search for him that I haven't done it again, and anyway, I don't know what I'd actually do if I found him. He's not exactly my hero or anything. I'm pretty angry with him if you must know.

I can't understand how he doesn't care about us at all. He must wonder how we're doing, or how big we are now. Sometimes, when I'm walking down the road, I look behind me in case he's following me, wearing dark glasses to disguise himself. Or I check

the trees in the park to see if he's hiding behind one, peeking out to see if I'm doing okay.

Worst of all, when I see Japanese men on the Tube (that's what the subway is called in London), I stare at them, wondering if they're my dad. I know what my dad looks like from photos and everything, but maybe he changed: grew a pointy beard, got fatter, got taller, changed his nose with plastic surgery, or something. Then I realize it's almost definitely not him because the man I'm staring at is, like, seventy and probably can't speak any English, and I know my dad is thirty-five and can.

My dad leaving feels like there's this massive black hole in me, like the ones up there in space. It twists in a dark, silent spiral, super heavy, sucking some of the good things in and swallowing them up. I don't know why it bothers me so much when I've lived nearly half my life without him but there are times when that black hole crushes me from the inside. But that's only sometimes.

BLACK HOLE

9

It's *molto* sad and everything but that's what happened. Nothing's perfect in this life, or so my mum
keeps telling me. So now you know a bit about me, I
can tell you how I got my genius idea and this whole
crazy story started.

TWO-DUE-NI

It was the last day of summer break, and I was starting Spit Hill Middle School the next morning. I can't say I was massively excited about going into middle school. There were loads of big loud scary kids in there—I used to see them coming out of the gate sometimes and getting on the bus. The girls looked even more dangerous than the boys. And in a few hours I was going to be walking through those gates myself. I was really freaking out about it. Maybe that's why I got the idea in the first place. Panic can make you do insane things—that's all I can say.

So that was the day Mum asked me go and pick up Bella from her friend's birthday party. It wasn't far, just a few streets past the park. The whole way I was

stressing about the disasters that could happen in school. What if no one liked me and everyone made new friends except me?

There were twenty-eight kids in my class in elementary school, and only twelve of them were girls. They were okay, and I hung out with them because I didn't really have much choice, but they weren't majorly good friends or anything. None of them liked art. Most of the boys were annoying and the three that were *almost* okay were going to other schools. So I really needed this middle school thing to work out. I was seriously hoping to make some new friends.

Because it was a new school and everything, it flashed across my mind to pretend I was someone else. I could say I was an orphan and my parents adopted me from Korea. Or that my father was a rock star, and I flew to LA every summer to hang out in my heart-shaped pool. But kids from my elementary school would be there, and they'd wreck my story. Everyone would laugh at me. Making a good first impression on your first day is important. If you mess up then, everyone ignores or ridicules you for the next seven years.

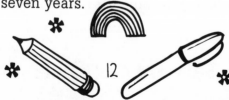

I nearly walked straight past Bella's friend's house because I was stressing so much. As soon as I stepped in the front door I saw Bella: you couldn't miss her. She was wearing this huge puffy pink party dress, white shiny shoes, and pink and white ribbons in her hair. She looked like a giant marshmallow. It was hard to believe we were even related. Her pigtails were bouncing up in the air, and she had chocolate smeared all over her mouth, her dress—everywhere.

I really didn't want to hold her sticky, chocolatey hands so I asked the party girl's mother if I could clean Bella up before we left. Seriously, if you had seen those hands you wouldn't have touched them either. But that might be just me. Me and muck have this thing. We just don't get along.

Once I'd washed her hands the best I could with her wriggling like an eel, I told Bella to wait outside so I could, you know, use the bathroom.

When I came out she was crying and rubbing her head.

"What happened?" I asked.

"That stupid Tommy Pyke," she wailed. "He ran up

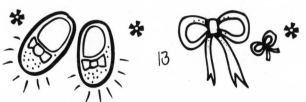

the stairs and pushed me over and I banged my head on the wall."

Tommy Pyke was only seven or something but he was *molto* violent, and he kept being mean to Bella. The first time was just after he joined our school, when he pulled her hair really hard and made her cry. Then he started tripping her on the playground and taking things out of her pencil case and throwing them at other kids in the class.

When we walked to the front door to leave the party, Tommy Pyke poked his head around the kitchen door and grinned. I took Bella's hand and gave him my evil death stare. That usually works on Bella, but he just stuck his tongue out at me and ran away.

On the way back home, with me holding Bella's hand which was now a bit clean but not extremely, we passed the playground.

A man was sitting in the sandpit playing with a little girl. The girl was only about two. She was pouring sand out of a plastic cup and talking to herself. Doing that at my age would be a *molto stupido* thing to do, and I was busy thinking about that when Bella stopped walking. She stood still, turned to the side, and looked at the little girl and her dad. She was still holding my hand and everything, but she just stood there watching them.

I tried to pull her away, but she didn't budge.

"Bella!" I said. "Come on, will you?"

But Bella didn't say anything. She just stood there, staring.

The little girl climbed all over her dad's legs, smearing sandy footprints on his trousers. It would have really bothered me but he didn't seem to mind. Then she plonked herself onto his lap. The little girl rested her head on her dad's chest, and he put his arms around her and stroked her hair.

Bella stood there gazing at them. I had to stand there too because I couldn't let go of her: I'd promised Mum I'd hold Bella's hand all the way home and I knew Mum would check. So we watched the man and his little girl, which is a weird thing to do if you think about it. The man looked up and his face was, like, "What?" but he didn't say anything.

I glanced at Bella, trying to figure out what she was doing. And then I saw it.

It was huge.

A gigantic, fat tear leaked out of Bella's left eye and rolled in slow motion all the way down her cheek until it fell off her chin and onto her marshmallow dress. Then another tear followed from her right eye.

I knew exactly what Bella was thinking: that little girl could sit on her daddy's lap, but Bella couldn't because she didn't have a daddy.

So I said, "Come on, Bella. Let's go."

And we walked home slowly, in silence.

The flat was quiet when we got in. Mum had a deadline, so she was working on her laptop in the sitting room. She told us to get something to drink until she finished, but Bella went to her room and I went to mine. I didn't even draw—and I always draw, especially when I feel bad. But I just lay on my bed and stared at the ceiling.

My room was pretty small, but at least I didn't have to share with Bella. Under the window was my desk with my drawing materials, which was my favorite place in the entire universe. On the right was my bed, a chest of drawers, and a small wardrobe. The walls were painted pale blue, and there were stars all

over my duvet and pillow covers. When I
turned off the lights, the glow-in-the-dark
comets and planets on the ceiling shone. I loved
my room. But even being in there didn't make me feel
any better.

Mum finished her work and called us to come out.
She made scrambled eggs for dinner but the gunk on
our plates looked more like clumps of wet toilet paper.
Bella and I sat at the small table in the kitchen and
stared at it. Neither of us felt hungry. Mum could tell
something was wrong because we were both so quiet
and Bella's the most unquiet person in the world.

After a while, Mum said, "Oh, come on. The eggs
aren't that bad."

But it wasn't the food.

Not this time.

I looked at Bella. She was staring at the plate and
her lips were twitching like she was going to cry
any second.

And even though she was a complete pain in the
butt, I felt sorry for her because now she knew what
the black hole felt like—the one my dad left behind
when he vamoosed. Maybe she'd felt it a bit before,

but the man in the park made her realize what I had known all along. Something major was missing. There was just this humongous hole where our dad was supposed to be. Someone we had completely trusted and loved had left us suddenly and never come back.

A thing like that can make you feel really small. And I didn't want to feel any smaller. It was bad enough wearing clothes for nine- to ten-year-olds when I was nearly twelve.

"Was the party that bad?" Mum asked, reaching across the table and lifting Bella's chin up. "Did Molly's mother lock you all in a cupboard? Because that's not a bad idea. We could do that at your party, Bella."

I didn't smile and neither did Bella. I knew Bella was thinking about the little girl in the park and so was I.

That little girl had a dad and we didn't.

He'd love her and look after her.

He'd make sure she didn't get bullied by nasty boys.

He'd tell her exactly what she needed to do to make a good impression on her first day at middle school. And he'd probably buy her a really cool phone as well so she wouldn't look like a cavewoman. (Dads just get

18

stuff like that. Mums, if they're anything like mine, just refuse to fork over their cash.)

It just didn't seem fair.

In the end, Mum gave up trying to force-feed us rubbery eggs and took our plates to the sink.

"What's going on, Amber?" she asked when Bella went to the toilet. "Anything I should know about?"

"Oh…err…not really. We just…we saw something a bit sad on the way home. It was a…um…this dead dog."

Mum looked at me suspiciously. "If there's anything wrong you can tell me, you know."

"Yeah, I know."

Except I couldn't tell her this. It would just make her feel bad. So I got up and went back to my room.

THREE-TRE-San

Before she went to bed, Bella knocked on my door. I was sharpening my pencils because I don't have any of those special mechanical ones for sketching yet, which is kind of annoying because I really need them. Bella came in wearing her matching pink nightdress, pink dressing gown, and pink slippers with Hello Kitty all over them. I just don't get why people like Hello Kitty. I know it's Japanese and supposed to be *kawaii* (cute) and everything, so maybe I should like it, but it's just a picture of a cartoon cat's head. I mean, seriously, what's the big deal?

Bella's hands were behind her back like she was hiding something. She looked much happier than she did when we got home from the party.

20

She moved her arms to the front and handed me a sealed envelope.

"What's this?" I asked, putting my sharpener down.

"Can you mail it for me tomorrow?"

I looked at the front of the envelope. There was nothing written on it.

"But it's blank, Bella."

"Yuuup."

"Who's it for?"

"None of your beeswax, Mrs. Nosy Pants."

"Um…okay. So you…you want me to put it in the mailbox?"

"Yes, Amber. Duuuh. That's what mailing means."

"But how is the mailman going to know who to give it to if it has no name on it?"

"Oh," she said, frowning.

She lay down on her belly on the floor and with her red crayon from the dollar store (well, she wasn't borrowing any of mine), she wrote on the front of the envelope: "TO MY DAD."

I looked at her.

"Bella—"

"Shush," she said. "Just mail it for me."

"But there's no address on it—"

"The mailman will know where he lives. He knows where everyone lives."

"He won't know where Dad lives. Nobody knows where Dad lives. Not even Mum."

"Didn't I say 'shush'? I'm sure I said 'shush.' Just mail it for me. Pleeease, Amber."

I sighed. What was I supposed to tell her? She was too little. She didn't get it. So I took it and put it on my desk, just to make her happy.

I know I shouldn't have done it and it's probably against the law and everything but when she went out of my room, I opened it.

✱   It said:

Dier Dad.
My nam is Bella and Im your dorta. My bithday party is on Sunday 16 Speptmbr and I rely want you too come. And I neid you to play with me in the park and posh me on the swing. Please come home
                love. Bella xxxx
P.S. Please buy me a perpel Swatch wach and Sparkle Girl Julerry Makar for my bithday.

✱

I didn't know what to do. Obviously, I wasn't going to mail it without an address on it. So instead, I put it in my secret place. If you pull the bottom drawer of my dresser all the way out, there's a space under it on the floor where I put my most sacred things. I had a coin that I found in Hyde Park that I'm sure is Roman or Viking and one day I'm going to sell it and get mega rich. I had a few other cool things in there too. Some of them are embarrassing, like key-rings I made out of lanyard strings when I was, like, seven and valentine cards my mum sent me. Stuff you can't exactly throw out but really don't want anyone to see. The letter wasn't one of my sacred things but where else was I going to put it?

I also had a picture of my dad holding me when I was a baby that I sneaked out of Nonna's album. Obviously, we have a whole bunch of photos of him in that album, but I wanted one for myself. One of him with me. Just to prove to myself that he did actually exist and hold me once, and he even looked proud. I don't look at that photo much because it makes me angry. I know it doesn't make sense to keep it, but there you go. Not everything makes sense. If it did, he would never have left in the first place.

There was another knock on my door, so I quickly closed the drawer.

"Hang on... Okay, you can come in now."

Bella stuck her head in.

"When do you think he'll get it?" she asked.

"Well, they have to find him first. It's not easy, you know. It takes teams of detectives *months* to find missing people."

She walked in to my room and said, "Oh," and did that thing where she points her toes inward and puts one foot over the other, like her toes are hugging.

"Do you think he'll get it before my birthday?"

"I don't know, Bella. I don't think so. But if by some weird miracle he did get it before then, I'm sure he'd come to your party."

Bella unhugged her toes and put her hands on her hips. "Amber?"

"Mmm?"

"How do you know I want Dad to come to my party?"

Oops.

"Well, it's kind of obvious, Bella. You did ask if he'd get it before your birthday."

"Oh," she said, frowning. "Hmm. Well, okay." And she skipped back to her room.

The letter wasn't my biggest problem at that point. I was so worried about starting my new school in the morning that I couldn't get to sleep for ages. When you can't sleep, your mind starts going a bit doolally. Well, mine does anyway. I start thinking all kinds of crazy things. And eventually the problem with Bella and her letter worked its way into my churning brain.

It was kind of mean and everything but there were times I really wished Bella wasn't my sister. But knowing there was a huge hole where our dad was supposed to be wasn't much fun either. The more I thought about it, the more I realized that maybe, just maybe, I could do something about it. I could save Bella from years of torture with one quick solution.

It seemed straightforward enough.

I decided to pretend to be my dad and write back to her, you know, to make her feel better.

And that was it.

Paff!

The most ingenious idea I've ever had lit up my mind like a firework.

FOUR-QUATTRO-ShI

I closed the door of my room, turned off the light, and switched on my flashlight because it made me feel focused and secretive.

I was on a mission.

I kicked off my shoes and sat on my bed, holding a piece of paper with an old sketch on the back. I wanted to write a rough draft first, because I was sure to mess up, and then copy the letter out on a clean piece of paper. It was easy enough to find scrap paper. I don't know if I told you this, but my room is full of drawings. I don't show them to anyone, but my mum has seen some obviously, because she comes into my room to clean and put my clothes away.

I draw all the time. It's my favorite thing to do in the entire universe, but it's kind of private. It's my thing and I don't feel comfortable showing it to anyone because that's like an invitation for them to tell me what they think. And then they'd get all phony and say it was really good and pretend they were interested. I actually don't really care what anyone thinks. Or maybe I do and that's why I keep it a secret. But, whatever, the point is, there's always paper I can recycle because drawing is my favorite thing ever.

To get in the right mood for writing this letter, I needed to think of my dad.

How else would I know what to write?

I tried to remember what he looked like, but my mind was blank. I got out the photo of him from under my drawer and stared at it. I thought it would trigger some memories but it didn't help. As hard as I tried, I couldn't really remember anything about him.

I remembered this kind of presence of him being around, but no specifics.

I couldn't picture his face in my mind or remember the sound of his voice. I couldn't remember him playing with me or dancing around the house to music. I

couldn't remember the shape of his hands or the feeling of being on his lap.

I couldn't remember him much at all.

All I had left of him was a fading memory and a flat, silent photo on a shiny piece of paper.

Weirdly, that felt good. Like I had a little blast of revenge. All I had was a 2D photo to remember him by. And unless he came back, that was all I'd ever have.

I figured that wasn't something any dad would be proud of.

So in a way, I was free. I could make him up exactly as I wanted.

I lay down because when I lie on my bed and stare at the ceiling, I get all my best ideas. Like glow-in-the-dark pencil lead for artists who want to draw late at night, or a neon sign for your forehead that changes with your mood, so people don't need to ask how you are all the time. I had the idea for my own style of drawing when I was staring at the ceiling: it involves layering drawings and cartoons and then painting and airbrushing on top. It's a whole new form of art and it'll make me world famous and blingingly rich. Artists everywhere will

love me because my brilliant ideas will make their lives easier and my art will be worth zillions. Then I'll have a glass ceiling so I can stare at the sky and the stars when I'm lying in bed. I'd have the best ideas then!

Anyway.

After a few tries I was happy with it, so I copied it onto a fresh piece of paper.

Dear Bella,

I can't come to your party because I'm on a top-secret mission. I can't tell you what it is because it would put you in danger, but it's to save the country and all so it's, like, way important. I can't tell you where I am either but one day, a long time from now, when all my missions are over, I might be able to come back. I might not though, so don't get all excited or anything.

I think about you both every day and if I could I would buy you both truckloads of presents and a cool phone for Amber and stuff.
Happy birthday!

Love,

DAD

I thought it was good. Not too much, not leading her on or anything. Just a little touch of him to make her feel better without her getting her hopes up.

I folded it up, put it under my pillow and lay down, feeling insanely happy.

I was a genius.

I'd win some big peace prize or a hero's medal or something.

I was a living legend.

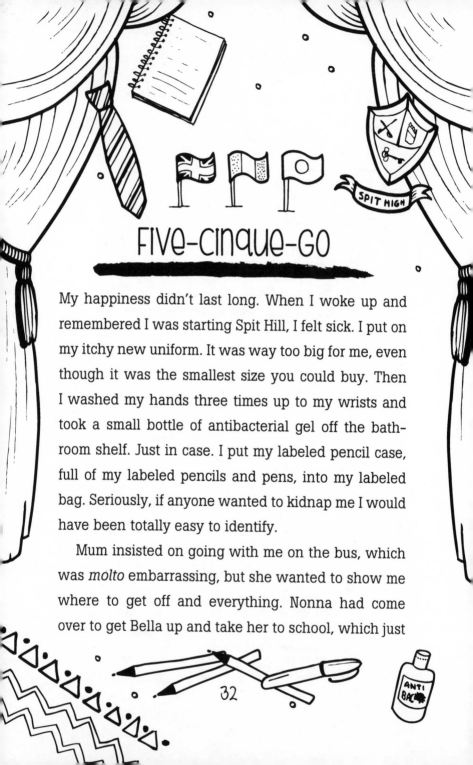

Five-Cinque-Go

My happiness didn't last long. When I woke up and remembered I was starting Spit Hill, I felt sick. I put on my itchy new uniform. It was way too big for me, even though it was the smallest size you could buy. Then I washed my hands three times up to my wrists and took a small bottle of antibacterial gel off the bathroom shelf. Just in case. I put my labeled pencil case, full of my labeled pencils and pens, into my labeled bag. Seriously, if anyone wanted to kidnap me I would have been totally easy to identify.

Mum insisted on going with me on the bus, which was *molto* embarrassing, but she wanted to show me where to get off and everything. Nonna had come over to get Bella up and take her to school, which just made the whole thing more stressful, because before I left, Nonna kissed me a hundred times like she was trying to suck my head off, took a hundred photos of me in my new uniform, and had to keep wiping tears from her eyes. You have to understand, she's Italian.

For my first journey to my new school, Mum was wearing a red-and-purple stripy cardigan with a thick furry hood and her hair was spinning like corkscrews off her head. I really wanted to sit far away from her but she was linking arms like I was her best friend so I couldn't escape. I had to get her arm off me though because other kids in the same uniform were looking at me and sniggering.

"So here's your stop, opposite the gas station—you're going to remember this tomorrow, aren't you?" Mum said when we got off the bus.

"Course."

"Do you want me to walk you to the gate?"

"Seriously, Mum, if you do, I'll never talk to you again."

"Don't tempt me," she said, grinning. Then she straightened my blazer collar and said, "Ahhhh, look at my little baby in her new uniform, all grown-up and going to big school."

33

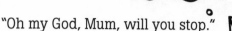

"Oh my God, Mum, will you stop."

"Fine, go on then. Good luck and all that. Don't get your head flushed down any toilets now, y'hear?"

Honestly. Instead of freaking me out, all she had to do was buy me an awesome phone so everyone would think I was cool. I didn't even have Internet on mine, and I just knew everyone else would be chatting with each other on WhatsApp all day long and posting photos of their lunches on Instagram. I had texts and calls and that was it. I'd be the laughing stock of sixth grade. To save me from lifelong shame, she only had to walk me into a phone shop. But did she? No. She did not. I even had fifty pounds of birthday money and although I needed a whole load of art stuff, I was saving up for a phone. I probably needed another fifty pounds at least to get what I wanted.

I walked into the main building wondering if I'd come out of there alive. What was the point of having my own Oyster card for the bus and a swipe card for the cafeteria when I was going to be eaten alive on my first day?

I saw Louise Newman and Melissa Atkinson and a

few friends from my old school but only Ben Haynes was in my grade. Obviously, I was the smallest in my entire year. I know this because we had assembly and I spent the whole time checking. If, like, a genie appeared, I'd seriously wish for someone in my year, just once, to be smaller than me.

Most of the morning we had to do these awkward "getting to know you" exercises with the other kids in our grade. I talked to a girl called Lulu Higgins and another called Sejal Shah and a boy called Hector and a bunch of others whose names I don't remember. But my one true friend did not stand out from behind a pillar and say, "Oh my God. *Finally.* I've found you! Let's be best friends our whole entire lives until we're seriously old and wrinkly and go on day trips to the seaside in buses and die on the same day." Which is kind of what I was hoping for.

This one girl attached herself to me though. Her name was Chloe Cain and she was all bouncy and giggly and oh-my-goshy. She was a whole head taller than me and had red hair, loads of freckles and super crooked teeth.

"Wow, you're sooo tiny," she said, which was not a great start to our friendship because it annoyed me immediately. "My brother's bigger than you and he's only nine. Are you *sure* you're supposed to be starting middle school? Did you skip a grade or something?"

"No. I'm just short."

"Oh. You look kind of Chinese."

That was the second most annoying thing she could have said. She was doing well.

"I'm half Japanese."

"Oh, that's so cool! Can you say something in Japanese?"

I hated it when people said that. I was trying to teach myself random words like *kawaii* (cute), *baka* (stupid) and *ohio gozimassu* (good morning) from Google Translate. And of course I knew my mum's number one Japanese phrase: *monku o itte mo haji-maranai desyo* (complaining won't change anything) but that was about it. Apart from being able to count. So I just said what I usually said.

"Sushi."

She cracked up and decided to tell me all about her life from the day she was born. She was nice and

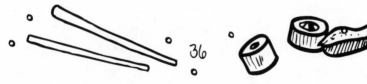

everything, but I wasn't sure I could ever be proper friends with her because her bag was pink and so was her pencil case. I know that's really shallow and everything, but she also had a button saying "I heart Justin Bieber" on her coat, and I really don't heart him at all, so our friendship was never going to be massively deep and special.

I tried to ignore her but she kept bouncing next to me at break and lunch to talk really fast and laugh every two seconds. It wasn't like there was anyone else to talk to though. I suppose I was kind of grateful for someone to sit with even if she did have a pink bag and a Justin Bieber button. I told myself, *Amber, it's not good to judge people. Maybe she got them from her big sister who was going to beat her up really badly if she didn't wear them, or something. You never know.*

After we finished lunch Chloe went bouncing off to introduce herself to another table of girls. She did it so easily. I'm rubbish at that. Being shy is pretty annoying. So I went to check out the art department instead.

The paintings and the ceramics in there were impressive, and there were some sculptures too, and some really cool screen prints. No one did the kind of

37

illustrations I did though, which was no surprise. I like being original, don't get me wrong, but sometimes I feel like a complete alien and wonder if I'll ever meet anyone from the same planet as me.

On the noticeboard there was a poster for an art competition. It sounded interesting and it had some really cool prizes but there was no way I was going to enter and expose myself like that. So I just wandered around until the bell rang and someone told me where I was supposed to be next.

There were good and bad things about my first day. I didn't say anything *stupido* in class and make an idiot of myself. And the teachers didn't shout too much, so that was good. But I got lost in that massive building with all the wings and the different floors, and I found out how much homework I was going to get every day, which was very, very bad.

It could have been worse, I suppose. It could have been better, obviously. I just felt so awkward. I needed guidance. I needed someone to tell me how to survive middle school and my mum was just, like, yeah, you'll be fine. But what if I wasn't? Then what?

Because we finished early, I went with Mum to pick Bella up from her first day back at my old elementary school, Parker Harris. Mum stayed in the car, and I went in to get Bella. The only reason I wanted to go was to show off. I had a Spit Hill uniform now. All those kids still at Parker Harris could see I was way, way above them because I was, like, a mature middle schooler now. My days of elementary school were sooo over.

But then something unexpected happened that messed my life up even more. I didn't know it then, obviously. You can never know these things in advance.

When Bella came out she was crying.

"Hey, what's the matter?" I asked.

"Tommy Pyke pushed me over and I hit my head on the door," she wailed.

All this rage welled up in me. It wasn't really about Bella: I was sick of being the shortest, and I'd had it with my horrible phone and my dad not being around and everyone thinking I was nine and Chinese, and all my rage just rolled up into one big ball. Rage can make you go a bit crazy. And there I was, in a middle-school uniform like a big kid, so the least I could do was act like one. So I held Bella's wrist (her hands were too grubby), walked back into the building and said, "Show me where he is."

Bella pointed him out. He was coming down the stairs so I waited at the bottom. He was tall for his age and pudgy too—maybe twice the size of Bella. He had a round, shaved head and dirty, inky fingers. He looked like he needed a serious scrub in a bath of disinfectant. He looked up at me like he wasn't sure what was going on. When he got down, I went up beside him, grabbed his arm, and twisted it behind his back really hard. Then I hissed in his ear, "Touch my sister again and I'll break your arm."

He was yelling so I let go of him, but not before I gave him my evil stare to show him I was serious. Then I took Bella's arm and walked out of there before any teachers came after me.

Bella didn't say a word but she had a huge grin all the way to the gate. Just before we got into the car, she whispered, "You're the best big sister in the whole wide world."

"Just don't tell Mum."

"Okay."

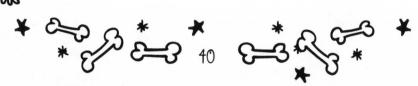

Then she climbed into the car and told Mum.

"You did *what*?" Mum shrieked, her eyes wide and scary.

"He deserved it, Mum."

"Amber, there's a fine line between standing up for her and bullying people. You have to be careful! You can't go around twisting people's arms and threatening to break them! That's bully behavior!"

I made a face at Bella but I didn't say anything. I just got out my hand gel and tried to rub the elementary-school bugs off my hands before I could go home and wash them properly.

Mum was freaked out because I never do anything like that, so when she got home she called Nonna and told her what happened.

"*Ambra? È vero?*" (That means, "Really? Is it true?")

"*Brava!*" Nonna bellowed. I could hear her laughing from where I was standing.

Mum frowned at me. I sat down on the sofa because I could just tell by her expression that it wasn't okay for me to disappear into my room and draw. Then she called up her friend Donna, whose son Hugo is my age, to ask what she thought of it.

"Wow," Donna said, "I wish Hugo was more like that!"

"Wait a minute here," Mum said, "am I the only one who thinks twisting someone's arm behind his back is not okay?"

"Yep," Donna said. "Good for Amber. That boy won't bother Bella again."

Mum put the phone down and looked at me, shocked. "No one else thinks that was out of order, Amber," she said. "But I'm still not convinced. I'm going to punish you for doing that. You have to realize that the best action in every situation is to talk. Violence is not the answer."

I wanted to argue that it wasn't *violence*: it was a matter of honor. But she was a mum so she just wouldn't get it.

"Can I choose my punishment?" I asked.

"No computer for a week."

"Noooo! Not that! Can't I have a different punishment?" I was reading this cool graphic novel online and they were showing their drawing techniques at the end of each chapter. I was really into it.

"No."

"*Tssshh.*"

Mum doesn't understand school stuff. I wasn't bullying him. I was defending my sister. I really don't know why I bothered though because it turned out to be nothing but trouble.

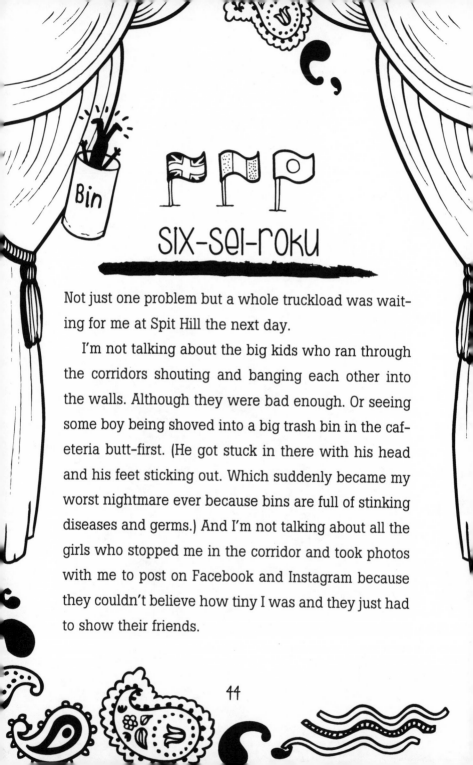

SIX-sei-roku

Not just one problem but a whole truckload was waiting for me at Spit Hill the next day.

I'm not talking about the big kids who ran through the corridors shouting and banging each other into the walls. Although they were bad enough. Or seeing some boy being shoved into a big trash bin in the cafeteria butt-first. (He got stuck in there with his head and his feet sticking out. Which suddenly became my worst nightmare ever because bins are full of stinking diseases and germs.) And I'm not talking about all the girls who stopped me in the corridor and took photos with me to post on Facebook and Instagram because they couldn't believe how tiny I was and they just had to show their friends.

I had three major problems by the time my first week was over.

It's embarrassing to admit it but the first problem was a boy. Boys just made me want to throw something at them before but this boy was almost okay. He was kind of small like me, not as short, obviously, but not exactly a basketball player either. He had messy dark hair that kind of flopped from his head, big brown eyes, and a spray of freckles on his face like they had been flicked off a paintbrush. He didn't seem loud and *stupido* like most of the others. I had to stand next to him a couple of times because he was getting stuff out of a locker right above mine.

Just standing there waiting for him to finish made me feel really awkward. It was the first time a boy had ever made me feel like that. And that was a problem because I was going to have to stand near him a few times a day, every day.

The second problem was a class.

Someone from Parker Harris must have arranged it because there it was on my schedule: period four, every week on Tuesday. It was called "Inward Reach" and the teacher's name was Miss Figgis. So

45

in period four, I went to the building, found the room, and sat down.

As far as I could make out, it was for kids whose parents were divorced or one of their parents was dead or the kids were, like, emotionally scarred by some major trauma or something. Miss Figgis had this mass of hair that looked like brown cotton candy and a really long face. She wore purple from head to foot and these dangly necklaces. I was sure she was going to catch one on a door handle and strangle herself. By the end of the class, I was kind of hoping she would.

In that first class she made us sit in a circle and take turns talking to the group about our feelings. It was right up there in the top ten most awkward situations of my entire life. I obviously didn't want to talk about my dad. Not in front of everyone, and especially not to her. She was the kind of person who would go on and on about it forever until you wished you'd never opened your big mouth.

Miss Figgis started by asking an eighth-grade girl called Hannah what she'd written lately in her diary about her father dying from cancer. Hannah was really nervous and shy and she started to whisper, "I

46

wrote...I wrote that—" but then she started crying and couldn't carry on. The last thing she needed, if you ask me, was to have to explain herself to a bunch of strangers who were staring out of the window yawning.

"You just take a moment to collect yourself, Hannah," Miss Figgis said, and she moved to the next person in the circle. "Joanne," she said to this meaty girl with dyed blond hair and fierce eyes, "why don't you tell us how you feel about your parents' divorce?"

Joanne rocked on her chair really hard and snarled, "Yesterday I smashed up everything in my bedroom with a tennis racket."

That's a pretty big clue, if you ask me.

So Miss Figgis spent a few minutes giving Joanne simple but effective tools she could use on a daily basis to deal with her anger.

"Joanne, sweetie, after me, take a deep breath to the count of five in through your nose: one...two... three...four...five...and release through your mouth slowly, like this: *foooooooooo*. Then breathe in through your nose again slowly to the count of five: one...two..."

Joanne's face slowly turned purple, and she kept rocking backward and forward on her chair. It looked like she was about to go right over. Miss Figgis just carried on breathing and counting, moving her hands up and down really slowly, and I was starting to feel sorry for Joanne because I would actually have died of embarrassment if that was me. But then she snapped and let out a sudden screech that was so loud I jumped six feet in the air. She grabbed things on the table—bags, pencil cases, water bottles—and started flinging them at the wall. A pencil case whizzed past Miss Figgis's ear. The rest of us sat there, frozen.

"Well, that's another way to release it, Joanne," Miss Figgis said, "but that's quite enough of that. Calm yourself down with some breathing, and I'll come back to you in a minute."

Joanne grabbed her bag and stormed to the door, yelling, "I'm getting out of this hellhole!" but Miss Figgis got up and called her back, reminding her that she couldn't leave because she was on report again, so she should just calm down and come back in.

Once Joanne was sitting down again, snorting with fury, Miss Figgis turned to me.

"Amber," she said super sweetly, "on behalf of the student welfare team, I'd like to welcome you to our 'Inward Reach' class. I hope you now have a sense of the wonderful atmosphere we've created here so you can talk with absolute safety and freedom about your innermost concerns."

I looked at Joanne scowling at me and Hannah sobbing into her hands in despair, and smiled weakly.

"Amber, would you like to tell us about yourself?"

I said politely, "No, thank you."

But Miss Figgis wasn't having it.

She obviously knew about my dad because she asked me a million questions about my family and how it was at home with my mum and my sister. I didn't say much, so she asked me if being "abandoned," by him made me feel worthless, which it didn't actually—not until she mentioned it anyway. And I hadn't ever really thought of being "abandoned," which

49

sounds miserable. Like a ghost town or a rusted-up car by the side of the road or something.

To get her away from that subject, I thought the best thing to do was just talk about something else. Maybe even make something up.

So I said, "You know how sometimes you wake up in the morning and you have this feeling like you're going to change the world?"

The others were squinting at me like, *no, we never feel like that. What are you going on about, freak?* But Miss Figgis was nodding so much, I thought her head was going to fall off and roll across the classroom.

"But then you have days when you wake up and you know you're never going to do anything great at all and there's all this darkness swirling in your head where murky thoughts grow?"

The other kids were making proper weirded-out faces now and Joanne was glaring at me like I'd just eaten an earthworm fresh from the mud, but Miss Figgis was still nodding excitedly.

"So when my head gets dark and murky, this huge, scary beast crawls out from under my bed. He's mas-sive and scaly and has these big horns and he stands over me, growling until I feel small and pathetic and want to stay in bed forever until I die."

I'm not great at making things up. Not when I'm being stared at by strangers and especially one who's potentially violent. It all got a bit too real actually. I only said all that stuff because I figured, as a psychologist, Miss Figgis would love it and stop talking about my dad. But it just made her worse. I really wished I hadn't mentioned it.

"Amber," she shrieked, "what a wonderful image! You are so in touch with your psyche—it's fabulously mature for someone your age!"

Joanne was kicking a chair leg over and over again, mouthing "stupid nerdy weirdo" at me. I decided there and then to stay well out of her way for the rest of school. Which was about the next seven years and counting.

"The beast is called *doubt*, Amber," Miss Figgis said. "Everyone questions their abilities. It's basically fear and you have to battle with it and overcome it because you can be anything you want to be. Search out those monsters, Amber! Shall we search out our monsters? Come

on, everybody up off your chairs and on to your hands and knees!"

She made us get on all fours and pretend we had flashlights in our hands, and we crawled around the room in a circle as she shouted, "Let's look under our beds for our monsters, shall we? Come on, everybody! Search under your beds for those monsters! Out! Out from under our beds, you horrible monsters!"

Everyone was giving me death stares for that little beauty. Even though Joanne refused to join in, I still wanted the ground to open up and swallow me.

Once we sat down again, to add to my misery, Miss Figgis said, "For those of you who are new, the wonderful news is that Spit Hill has an art competition every year. The deadline for this year's art competition is next Wednesday, and it's a big deal here at Spit Hill. The older students have known about it since Easter and many have been working on their submissions over the summer. The theme this year is 'What Matters to Me.' I know it's short notice, but I want each of you to bring in a picture next week of something that's important to you. I'm going to enter each and every one of you into the competition."

INWARD
REACH

I shrank in my chair.

Oh. My.

There was no way on earth I was showing *anyone* my secret art or having it judged in some school competition.

And then, when I thought the class had got as bad as it could possibly be, we all had to hold hands and sing "I am beautiful in every single way..."

I was so glad when it ended. But it was a temporary type of gladness because it was on my schedule and I was going to have to go in there next week and the week after that. There was no avoiding it. And to top it all, Miss Figgis wanted a picture from each of us for the art competition.

How the *Phineas and Ferb* was I going to get out of that?

AMBER

SEVEN-SETTE-SHICHI

Bad as that class was, it wasn't even the worst of my problems. Nonna says "there's never a two without a three," meaning problems always come in threes. I don't know if it's true but my third problem at Spit Hill turned out to be my biggest problem of all.

Wednesday wasn't any better than Monday or Tuesday. I forgot the books I was supposed to bring in. I listened to teachers go on and on about how much work we needed to do. I got lost in school. At break I sat with Chloe and some other girls who asked me what kind of phone I had and tried not to laugh when I told them. Then they all chatted about how much they wanted to marry Justin Bieber.

I *tried* to speak to other people in my class but I felt awkward and shy and didn't know what to say after the usual, "Hi, I'm Amber. Yes, I'm really eleven. No, I'm not Chinese, I'm half Japanese and half Italian. Sushi."

After school, Mum made me go with her to pick Bella up from her after-school dance class. I'm sure Bella only went to ballet so she could wear a pink tutu.

Anyway.

I walked into the school and saw Tommy Pyke in the playground wearing a soccer jersey. He was running toward the goal with the ball under his arm and the other boys were shouting, running after him, and trying to get it off him. I don't know much about soccer, but I'm pretty sure that's not the way you play.

I asked Bella if he'd been mean to her again and she said no. I must say, I felt pretty heroic and brave and all those things I never usually feel because bending people's arms behind their backs is not something I tend to go around doing. I'm a skinny scaredy-cat and people can see it a mile away. But I'd stood up for my annoying sister. I had taken action. I was a fearless warrior.

I was the coolest sister alive.

I was herding Bella out of there and toward the car when I saw something that rammed my fear straight back in me again.

Guess who walked into the playground as we were walking out?

Yep, Joanne. The wild and violent girl from my Inward Reach class who'd wrecked her bedroom with a tennis racket.

And guess who ran up to her with the ball under his arm?

Tommy Pyke.

My stomach did a flip.

"Um...who's that girl with Tommy Pyke?" I asked Bella, thinking all the while, *Please don't say she's his big sister. Please.*

"Oh, that's his big sister. She's super scary."

I felt something inside me die. All my blood must have drained down to my feet because I felt faint and my shoes got really heavy. I scooted Bella across the playground to get out of there, and at the last minute, I turned to look at them. Tommy was telling Joanne something and pointing at me. She looked over at me and nodded slowly.

I felt my eyes spring wide open in fear and panic. Of all the people I could have tried out my bravery on it had to be her brother!

On no. Oh God. My insides clamped tight in panic. She was so massive and so scary and I suddenly wished I had that superhero ability to grow gigantic and have rippling muscles and a roaring voice and not be tiny and terrified and squeak like a gerbil. I scurried in horror to the car, mentally kicking myself for not being super tough and a master at self-defense. Instead I was small and useless and about to suffer a painful and torturous death.

Why? Why wasn't there a Super Mighty Amber who grew a hundred feet tall and kicked some serious butt? Why wasn't there a small but hard-core ninja warrior Amber hiding beneath my uniform?

But no. None of those other Ambers existed.

There was just me.

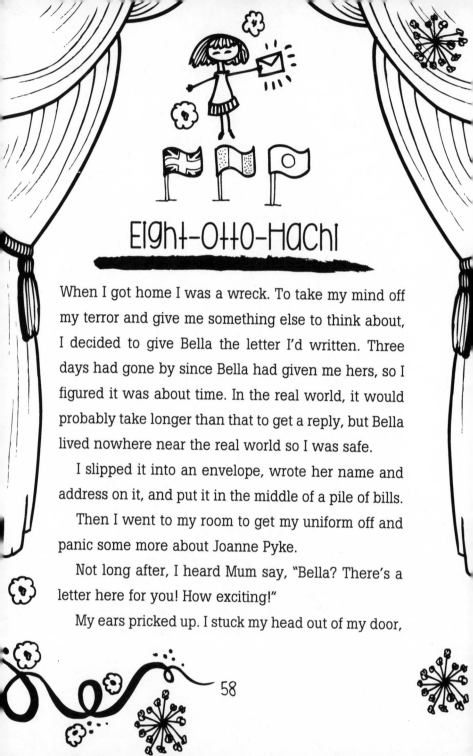

Eight-Otto-Hachi

When I got home I was a wreck. To take my mind off my terror and give me something else to think about, I decided to give Bella the letter I'd written. Three days had gone by since Bella had given me hers, so I figured it was about time. In the real world, it would probably take longer than that to get a reply, but Bella lived nowhere near the real world so I was safe.

I slipped it into an envelope, wrote her name and address on it, and put it in the middle of a pile of bills.

Then I went to my room to get my uniform off and panic some more about Joanne Pyke.

Not long after, I heard Mum say, "Bella? There's a letter here for you! How exciting!"

My ears pricked up. I stuck my head out of my door,

went into the corridor and pretended I was looking for something in my coat pocket.

Bella's feet went skidigiddigiddy across the floor and she arrived with huge eyes at Mum's side.

"There's no return address on it," Mum said, turning it over with a scrunched-up face.

Bella was trying to tug it out of her hands. "Oh, that's okay," she said.

"Wait, Bella—do you know what it is? Maybe I should open it."

"I know what it is," Bella said, "but it's a secret."

Mum put her hands on her hips and raised her right eyebrow. She does that when she's suspicious. She lifts her right eyebrow like it's being tugged by an invisible string above her head. I've tried and tried, but I can't do it without the other eyebrow jumping up too, which is so annoying.

"A secret, huh?"

Mum lifted her eyebrow again. *Why?! Why can't I do that?!*

"Yep," Bella said.

"I don't think I like your secret," Mum said, folding her arms. "Is it a birthday invitation from a friend at school? Because if it is, I'll have to write it on the calendar, otherwise you'll miss it."

"No, Mummy," Bella said, taking one of my mum's hands in hers. "You don't have to worry. It's about MY birthday party."

Mum smiled. "Well, okay then," she said and went to cook dinner. Bella looked so happy. She ran off with the letter to her room and closed the door.

It really tickled me to see how excited she was. This was totally going to sort out everything because now she'd stop thinking our dad was about to turn up. But I couldn't hang around to see her reaction because just then, Nonna arrived to look after her so Mum could take me to karate.

Karate was a pretty new thing in my life. There were three reasons I wanted to go. One was that it was Japanese so it connected me to my roots and everything. Not that anyone else there was Japanese. Even the instructor was, like, Greek or Turkish or something. Genetically, you'd think I'd be good at karate, being half Japanese, like the secrets of speed and flexibility had trickled into my DNA over the centuries. But if that was true, nothing had revealed itself yet.

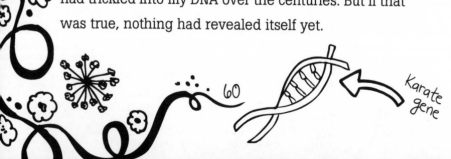

Karate gene

The second reason was that I was a skinny coward and I was kind of hoping it would make me muscley, powerful and fearless. Because—and this was the third reason—I needed to protect myself. At first, it was in case my mum got sick or died or something and Bella and I had to live on the streets. I didn't tell my mum that was why I wanted to do karate, obviously. But I had to think about these things. After my dad left, I realized I had to have a plan in case we woke up one morning and she was gone too. What if she didn't come home from work one day? Then what?

But now I had another reason. I really wished I'd started karate when I was, like, three days old and not waited until I was eleven. That Joanne girl was going to hunt me down. I was so dead. Why oh why did I wait so long?

I was only a white belt and—surprise, surprise—I was the smallest one there. There was an eight-year-old who was bigger than me, plus two girls and six boys who all thought they were cool but obviously weren't, even though two of them had green belts already. I wasn't that good or anything but I needed to be a master as soon as possible. It seemed like a long shot, but I was praying for a miracle.

After we did the warm-up our teacher did this exercise where he tried to hit us with a big soft baseball bat. We had to duck or jump up to get out of the way, and we had to be *molto veloce* or we'd get whacked by it. I wasn't sure whether that was important because in Japan people chased each with big soft baseball bats or what, but I didn't want to ask in case it was a stupid question. I was Japanese—I was the one who needed to know stuff like that. If my dad had been around he'd have known. Honestly. All this crucial information was now a mystery to me.

"Amber, it doesn't break bones, you know," my instructor said as I flinched and squealed to get out of the way. "Stop being such a chicken."

But I couldn't because it was scary. It might have been a soft batty thing but he was a huge hairy karate teacher. I was a tiny girl. I was sure he would, like, squash me to death so, trust me, I ran fast. He didn't catch me. But I just know he'll try harder next time.

After that we practiced this *kata* we're learning, which is a series of moves. That was okay because no one was trying to hit me. But it didn't make me feel any better. I sucked at karate. I wanted to be awesome

but I was small and scared of everyone and everything that came near me, especially the instructor.

Becoming a master was not going to be easy.

When I got home Nonna started going on at me again for wearing the same striped black-and-white top and black hoodie every single day of my life.

"*Ambra, perché indossi il nero?*" she asked, waving her fingers in front of her the way Italians do when they're trying to make a point. I knew it meant "why are you wearing black?" but I pretended I couldn't understand her. She carried on anyway. "Why this *brutta*, dirty *felpa* (ugly, dirty hoodie) that boys and robbers wear? *Non è carino.* (It's not nice.) *Sei una bella ragazza*, Ambra. You beautiful girl. I buy you new cloz, yes?"

"No thanks, Nonna."

I always said no because you could just bet your life she would buy something really disgusting. Last time it was a yellow dress with lace and butterflies. Besides, my hoodie wasn't dirty. I put it in the wash even when I wore it for five minutes because my clothes, like my hands, had to be *molto* clean.

You should see my nonna though. She's always really glamorous. Just to come and babysit, she wears swishy stylish clothes that match and a massive ring and bracelet. Her nails are always painted; her dyed-blond hair is always perfectly blow-dried; and she wears fancy Italian shoes and a swishy coat with a furry collar. You have to understand: she's Italian and there are Italian women who look like that even when they're gardening and cleaning the toilet.

"Is Bella still in her room?" I asked. Bella didn't ever spend time alone in her room. She liked being with people, mainly so she could boss them around.

"She come out but now she go back in," Nonna said. *"Digli di lavarsi i denti."*

So I went to tell Bella her to brush her teeth and check up on her. My letter should have sorted her out and made her understand everything. Maybe she was sad about Dad not turning up but it was for the best.

"Bella?" I called out. "Can I come in?"

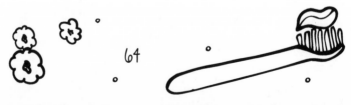

64

"No."

"Oh. Everything okay?"

"Yes," called the muffled voice from the other side of the door. I strained to hear but I couldn't tell if she was happy or what.

"Want to play something?"

"I'm busy. Maybe later."

She was probably making a bracelet. She had this kit to make these ugly plastic bracelets with dangly things hanging off them. They took her ages to make. I wouldn't be seen dead in one but she really liked them.

"Oh. Okay. Nonna said brush your teeth."

"After."

"Okay."

I had a shower, got my pajamas on, and knocked on her door again.

"Everything okay in there?" I asked again.

"Yep."

She opened the door. She looked so happy and excited. It totally confused me.

"What was that letter all about, Bella? Was it from

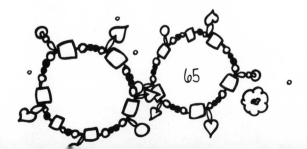

Dad? You can tell *me*—I'm the one mailing your letters for you, don't forget."

"It's top secret."

"And you can't even tell me?"

She thought about it. She stuck out her lips and twisted them to one side. She squinted her eyes at me. Then she said, "Hmm. Well, if you must know, yes. It is from Dad. He told me something but you have to promise not to tell anyone."

"Fine, I promise, just tell me."

"But do you promisey promise?"

"What? What does that mean?"

"It's a promise with an extra prom-isey bit to make sure."

Sigh.

"Yes, Bella. I promisey promise with the extra promisey bit."

She raised herself up on tiptoes, put her hands around her mouth, and whispered in my ear, "Dad is actually a king, and I'm a very important princess. And he's going to come to my birthday party."

I pulled back and stared at her with my mouth

open. What could I say? I couldn't exactly say, "Hey, wait a minute—that's not what I wrote at all!"

Instead I stammered, "What? That…that can't be true, Bella! For a start there's no king in *Japan*—"

"I didn't say he was the King of Japan—"

"So where, then? That's where he was from—"

"I told you. It's a secret. Maybe he'll tell you at my birthday party."

"Bella, he's not coming to your birthday party."

"Yes, he is."

"No, he isn't. You sure he said that?"

"Yep."

"Surey sure?"

"Surey surey extra super surey sure."

And she danced down the hall to brush her *denti.*

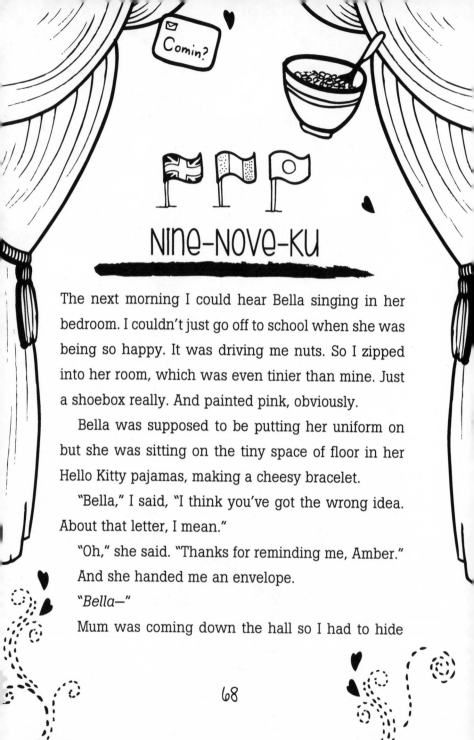

NINE-NOVE-KU

The next morning I could hear Bella singing in her bedroom. I couldn't just go off to school when she was being so happy. It was driving me nuts. So I zipped into her room, which was even tinier than mine. Just a shoebox really. And painted pink, obviously.

Bella was supposed to be putting her uniform on but she was sitting on the tiny space of floor in her Hello Kitty pajamas, making a cheesy bracelet.

"Bella," I said, "I think you've got the wrong idea. About that letter, I mean."

"Oh," she said. "Thanks for reminding me, Amber." And she handed me an envelope.

"*Bella—*"

Mum was coming down the hall so I had to hide

it up my shirt. I knew Bella was going to get in loads of trouble because she had to leave for school in five minutes and she was still wearing pink, had wild hair, and hadn't eaten breakfast yet.

I zipped out of the door just as Mum arrived, saying, "Please tell me she's dressed."

I gave Mum the kind of grin that meant "Yeah, right" and ran away just as Mum went into Bella's room and started roaring.

At the table I guzzled my cereal nervously.

What was in this new letter under my shirt?

Ba ding. I got a text. From Chloe Cain.

Goin 2 bus stop. Bus in 4 mins. Comin?

It turned out that Chloe lived, like, three streets away so she'd been super excited about going to school together every day. I wasn't dying of happiness about it or anything but she did have this app on her phone that told her exactly when the bus was coming. It was so cool. She could plan when to leave the house so she could get there exactly when it arrived. Cavegirl losers like me had no idea of bus times, so we missed it and then had to wait decades in the wind and the rain for the next one. Like in the Olden Days.

Mum was still yelling at Bella to get dressed so I sent Chloe a text back.

comin.

I read Bella's letter as soon as I was out of our house.

Dier Dad,
Shal I wer the ornge and green dresse to my party or dresse up as a unicorn? Nonna seys she has a unicorn coustume for me. What do you think?

Love, Bella
xxx

This was bad.

Wait.

Unicorn costume?

I couldn't imagine my nonna buying a unicorn costume. She just wasn't that type of nonna. She was the kind who would buy a fairy costume or one of those flouncy princess dresses. If you ask me, that's where

Bella gets all her ideas about being a princess from. Grandmas are really good at messing up a kid's grip on reality.

You could never tell with Nonna though. Her English wasn't great so she got things wrong all the time. Last year, she phoned to tell me she bought me a badger for my birthday. Mum overheard me saying, "You bought me a *badger*?" and freaked out. She yelled, "tell her she can't bring it over here! We can't keep a badger in a flat! It's not even legal to own one as a pet. They're dangerous!"

So I told Nonna but she said, "*Chiacchiere!* Nonsense! I coming now. *È carino*. He very sssweet. I show you, no?" She insisted they were good pets and she had already bought it, along with a lovely cage, so there was nothing to argue about and she was bringing it round.

When Nonna turned up she was holding a cage.

We all stared at it.

In the cage was a small green budgie.

Even Mum thought that was hilarious. I took it back to the pet shop though because it makes me sad to see birds in

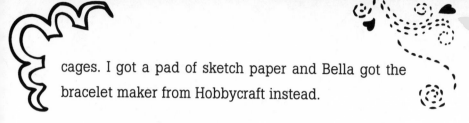

cages. I got a pad of sketch paper and Bella got the bracelet maker from Hobbycraft instead.

On the way to school, Chloe was talking and talking, but I really didn't hear anything she said. My head was burning up with stress and confusion. I wanted to take it off and leave it somewhere to cool down.

Now Bella thought Dad was coming to her party. It was a catastrophe. Why had I written back to her?

On top of that, I'd done a brilliant job of ruining middle school before the very first week was out.

I went through the gates feeling ill.

I kept my head down all morning. I didn't see Joanne Pyke. It's not like she's in my grade or any-thing. I spent most of my morning classes racking my brain to find solutions and turn it all around.

To start with, I pleaded with my guidance counse-lor, Mrs. DeLuca, to let me drop Miss Figgis's class, but she said it was mandatory for certain students and I was one of them.

I looked up the word "mandatory" in a school dictionary during break and it means "you have to, sucker; you have no choice," which was *molto*

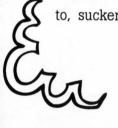

depressing news. Actually, that's not exactly what it said in the dictionary, which is a shame. Imagine how cool it would be if the dictionary actually said things like that!

Then the break ended, and I had to go to my classes. Middle school is annoying because there are all these completely random subjects like history and French and geography and none of them seem very useful. I don't know why they insist on teaching you all this stuff you'll forget as soon as you walk out of the door. What about teaching you how to get out of doing things you don't want to do? Or sorting out complicated messes and getting violent girls off your back? But noooo. Instead we learn algebra, which isn't going to help much when I'm traumatized about my classes for kids with trauma.

When I went to put my stuff away, I saw Locker Boy again. As soon as I saw him, I did an about-face and stood at the window pretending to watch the caretaker cut the grass. I put Locker Boy to the back back backest part of my mind. He was the least of my problems. But I had to admit, he was a problem. I have no idea why, but when I saw him, my brain went "aaahhhhh, nice thing" like it does when it sees chocolate cake smothered in thick chocolate icing, and not "ew, yucky thing" like it does when it sees doggy doo or snotty tissues.

At the end of school, when I was coming out of the gate, Joanne was up ahead of me with a group of big kids. Luckily, she was a bit far away or I'd have been in serious trouble. She turned around and looked at me. Then she smiled the coldest, most dangerous smile I've ever seen in my entire life and at that moment I knew it. I was going to need more than a few karate *katas* to get out of this one.

Ten-Dieci-Jū

After dinner, when Mum was helping Bella with her science homework and trying not to scream because Bella can't concentrate to save her life, I went into my room and closed the door.

It was all getting too much.

I was trying not to panic but I felt terror rise up in me like water filling a sinking ship, which I know about because I watched *Titanic* with Nonna. She cried so much she used half a box of tissues. I think it reminds her of Nonno (my grandpa), who died in a car accident before I was born. But anyway.

My heart was aching and my head was dizzy. I needed to talk to someone about it or I was going to explode. I couldn't tell my mum this huge scary girl was after me because she'd say "Well, yeah, that's what happens when you go around bending people's arms back." She'd tell me I'd made my bed and now I had to lie in it, or one of those other expressions that just don't make any sense.

Nonna would shout to the whole street from the window to call the police or say something super dramatic and super unhelpful, like, "Anyone come near my grandchildren, I kill him and all his family!"

I didn't really have any proper friends to help me. And Bella was, well, Bella.

And then I thought about the little girl in the park. She had her dad.

Where was my dad when I needed him?

If ever there was a time when I needed him, it was now.

I walked over to my dresser, pulled the bottom one all the way out and put it to one side. I reached into the space underneath it and took out the photo of my dad.

I stared at it.

And for the first time in as long as I could remember, I didn't feel angry with my dad. I didn't hate him

for leaving or have dark, evil thoughts brewing as I looked at his photo.

I missed him.

I couldn't remember any details about him but it didn't matter.

He was my dad. I remembered him being there. And I suddenly missed him so much I felt the black hole inside me growing and growing and crushing me so much I could hardly breathe.

I put the photo back and closed the drawer. Then I went over to my bed, laid on it, and curled up in a ball. A tight, tight ball like a hedgehog. And I lay there wishing my stress would zoom through the air like radio waves to wherever my dad was. And he'd come home to help me.

Ages went by. Maybe even twenty minutes.

He didn't knock on the door.

The black hole grew just a bit more until it pressed on my throat.

He was gone.

There was only one thing that could help me breathe and stop the ache.

I lifted myself up, black hole and all, wiped my

77

eyes, and got a pad of sketch paper from my desk. I took my favorite 2B pencil out of the pencil jar and sat on the floor with my legs crossed. I already felt better, just sitting like that. Drawing sorts me out because I can draw the world better than it is. And if any situation needed to be better, it was this one.

My pencil started moving on the page. I didn't think. I just drew. It was like my hand took over without my brain getting involved.

After a while, the lines on the page started looking like a leg. It grew and lines appeared above it. In a short while I noticed there was an arm and then another one. All attached to a big, strong body. And a head. I looked down at the strange thing that had appeared on the paper.

It was a big, strong protector of a dad. He stood tall and proud. Wearing a cape and a mask.

It was kind of weird, seeing him there suddenly. It made me grin. So I said, "Hey."

I imagined the person in the drawing answering me.

"Hey yourself. What's up?"

"Oh, you know. This and that."

And then the idea of him kind of grew.

I flipped over the paper so I had a fresh piece and sketched him again, adding details and making him more real. I kept the mask and the cape though.

And before I knew it, he started to come to life.

I stared at the paper.

It made me feel really happy. And the more I thought about it, the more I liked the idea of a made-up dad.

Real dads get tired and grumpy. They're always at work, but, like, *always*. Most of them have no idea about the secret techniques of top karate moves. Some of them get drunk and yell. Loads of them have bad backs and complain all the time. Worst of all, they can be seriously unimaginative so they don't ever offer to take you kite-surfing. They can be nice and all, I'm not saying all of them are like that.

But this dad of mine was perfect.

He was always there for me.

I could talk to him about anything.

He always had time to hang out.

He had money, which is important because dads have to be able to buy you stuff.

He knew how to do everything really well and he was a mountain of fun.

He would look after me.

And he would never, ever leave.

He was everything a dad should be.

And because it suddenly felt so amazingly good to have him there, I decided to try something out. I got another piece of paper, took a deep breath, and drew him sitting in my room with me.

The perfect dad.

It was so cool!

And then another idea came to me. I closed my eyes and imagined the dad in my illustration didn't just exist on paper. I imagined he was sitting on the end of my bed.

And there he was, real as anything.

So I talked to him.

It went like this.

"I've complicated my life so badly that I don't even want to get up tomorrow morning," I said.

"Okay," you said, "but you can't start a story half-way through. You have to start at the beginning and tell me everything."

"Everything? Who says?"

"Me."

"Okay. What do you want to know?"

"Start at the beginning," you said, stretching and getting comfortable.

So I began.

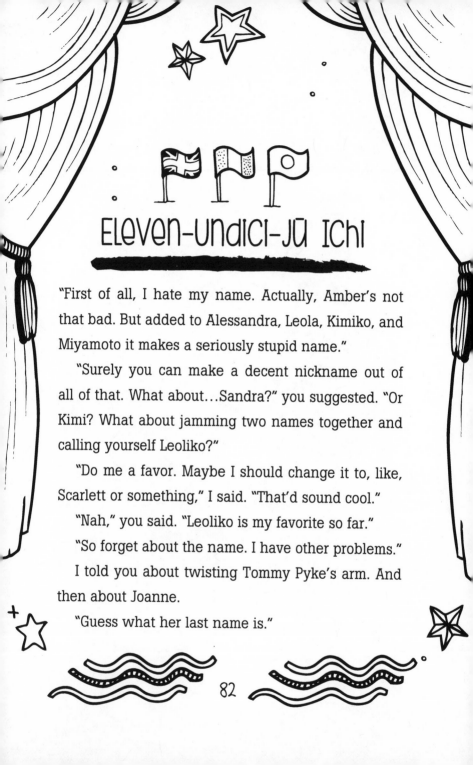

Eleven-Undici-Jū Ichi

"First of all, I hate my name. Actually, Amber's not that bad. But added to Alessandra, Leola, Kimiko, and Miyamoto it makes a seriously stupid name."

"Surely you can make a decent nickname out of all of that. What about…Sandra?" you suggested. "Or Kimi? What about jamming two names together and calling yourself Leoliko?"

"Do me a favor. Maybe I should change it to, like, Scarlett or something," I said. "That'd sound cool."

"Nah," you said. "Leoliko is my favorite so far."

"So forget about the name. I have other problems."

I told you about twisting Tommy Pyke's arm. And then about Joanne.

"Guess what her last name is."

"Wong?"

"Pyke. And now she's seriously out to get me."

You didn't seem that worried about Joanne.

"Just twist *her* arm as well," you said.

"I can't. She's huge and violent. She'll kill me."

"Nah. We'll show her who's boss."

I didn't like to remind you that you weren't real and I was kind of on my own once I got to school.

I told you about Miss Figgis's class and how bad it made me feel and how much I hated it. I told you about Locker Boy and how he made my blood fizz so not enough oxygen got to my brain when he was around. I told you about the black hole my dad left behind and how it made me think dark, murky thoughts and a beast was growing in all that darkness and had moved in under my bed—a big, scary beast that came out when I was feeling small and scared and rubbish at everything, and snorted and growled and made me feel worse.

And then, last but not least, I told you about Bella and the letter.

You listened.

And you listened.

I told you everything.

You didn't say anything for a while. I suppose you were digesting it.

Eventually you said, "Whoa. You're in deep slime, my friend."

It made my heart sink.

"What do I do? She thinks our dad is coming to her party! And she thinks he's the king of somewhere and she's the princess!"

"Tricky. So what do you need?" you asked. "I mean, from me. What do you need me to do?"

I sat up. "I could really do with some help sorting this mess out," I said. "For starters, I want to be a fearless warrior—a black belt, whatever *dan* karate master—and not a complete chicken. Because I truly believe a fearless warrior is buried deep inside me just waiting to break free, but it must be down very deep. And I wish she'd appear because I really don't want that girl Joanne to beat me up or give me a hard time at school."

"Course you don't. Is that it?"

"Well, it would be quite cool to talk to that boy by my locker—just to make friends. And meet a proper

friend: one who I like hanging out with and who likes hanging out with me. It would be great to feel whole for once and not half this and half that with one half of me missing."

You nodded. "Ooookkkaaaaaay."

"While you're at it, you know the black hole that swirls about when I think of my dad? Well, can you make it go away? Not to mention the beast under my bed. Oh, I seriously, seriously need a new phone. And last of all, Bella has to get that our dad isn't coming to her party."

You blew out a long, slow whistle. "Not asking for much, then, are you?"

I hung my head. Even with my dream dad by my side, I was asking for the impossible.

"Nothing's impossible," you said, as if you were reading my mind. It was pretty impressive, I have to say.

"Really? Do you mean that?"

"Well, except surviving without food or water for ten years, uncracking an egg, having a conversation with a horse in Spanish, teaching a legless man to tap dance—"

"I get the picture. So will you help me?"

"Why do you think I'm here?"

A tsunami of relief whammed through my entire body. "Oh, wow! That's so great! Where do we start?"

"We start with Bella. You're going to have to write back to her. And this time tell it to her straight."

I nodded. *Of course!* I got out a pen and paper and began straight away.

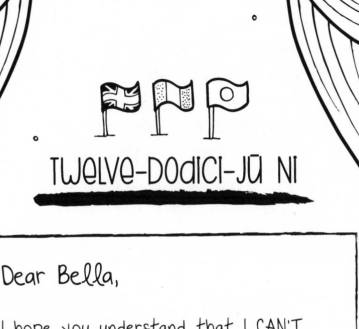

TWELVE-DODICI-JŪ NI

Dear Bella,

I hope you understand that I CAN'T COME TO YOUR BIRTHDAY PARTY. I have to do a VERY IMPORTANT MISSION like I said before and there's NO WAY ON EARTH I will be there. At all. Absolutely and definitely not.

I'm just a REGULAR person, the most NORMAL NON-ROYAL sort of person, nothing special, definitely NOT RICH or IMPORTANT in any way at all and very boring apart from the missions I have to do from time to time which mean I CAN'T COME TO YOUR BIRTHDAY PARTY.

Are you sure it's a unicorn costume?

I won't get to see it anyway because I CAN'T COME.

But I hope you have fun.

Love,

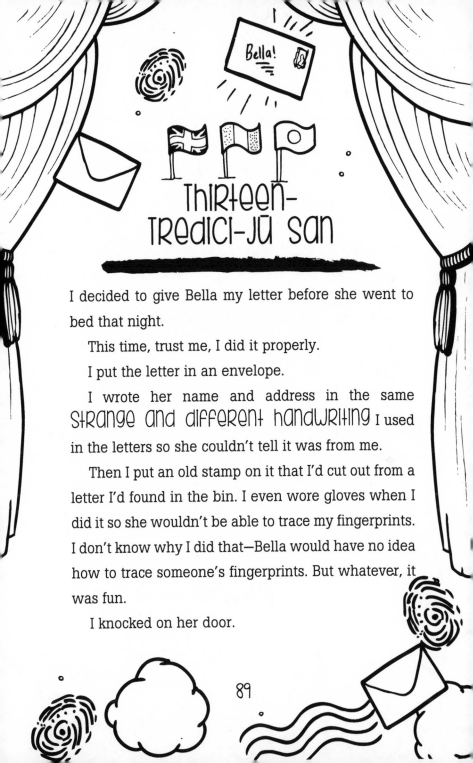

Thirteen-
Tredici-Jū san

I decided to give Bella my letter before she went to bed that night.

This time, trust me, I did it properly.

I put the letter in an envelope.

I wrote her name and address in the same **STRANGE AND DIFFERENT HANDWRITING** I used in the letters so she couldn't tell it was from me.

Then I put an old stamp on it that I'd cut out from a letter I'd found in the bin. I even wore gloves when I did it so she wouldn't be able to trace my fingerprints. I don't know why I did that—Bella would have no idea how to trace someone's fingerprints. But whatever, it was fun.

I knocked on her door.

"I'm asleep!" she shouted.

I opened the door and stuck my head in. She slept with a low light on because she was afraid of the dark, so I could see her lying in bed. Maybe she had a beast living under her bed as well—I'd never thought of that before.

Her eyes were closed so tightly together, they were straining and fluttering.

"I know you're not asleep, Bella. And you won't want to be when you see what I've got here."

She opened her eyes a tiny bit so her face was still squished up.

"You got another letter. I found it on the doormat."

Luckily, Bella has no idea that the mailman doesn't deliver letters at night.

She jumped out of bed and tried to snatch it out of my hands, but I held it up high and got her to look right into my eyes.

"If it's from Dad, you have to tell me what it says, okay? But really—everything he says, word for word."

"There might be things that I can't tell you," she said, jumping up to grab it. "Secrets. Between me and him."

90

"Bella—"

"Okay, okay."

I handed it to her and went out.

She had to get the message this time.

It was late and I hadn't done my homework.

For French I had to name the things in my room, like my bed and my lamp. Except I didn't speak French so how was I supposed to know what they were called?

In math I had to multiply fractions. Just the thought of it made my brain shrivel up and hide behind my ear.

And for art I had to draw an apple.

So obviously I started with the apple.

I got the last one from the bowl, which was a bit wrinkly, and laid it on the kitchen table. Then I moved the usual pile of letters and books and bits of rubbish so I wouldn't have to draw them too. The light was okay—it was dark but the main light was on and it cast a shadow over the wood.

While I was drawing it, I thought about Bella.

Was she going to be devastated that Dad wasn't coming to her party?

Was she always going to be that loopy?

Did Nonna really buy her a unicorn costume?

Chloe texted me to ask about the French homework so I told her the page number and went back to drawing the apple. She texted me three more times but I ignored her because I was busy. I don't mind drawing apples for art homework: it's not like handing in my own artwork, which is *molto* personal. A drawing of an apple? Even I could deal with that.

I don't know how it happened but suddenly Mum was yelling, "Amber! Go and get ready for bed!"

I looked at the clock. *Oops.*

I hadn't done my French or math. But my apple looked pretty good.

I crept past Bella's room because she was supposed to be asleep by that time. But she opened the door of her room suddenly as I walked past and made me jump.

"Whoa, you scared me," I said. "What are you doing?"

"Going to the *toilet.*"

She didn't look sad. Quite the opposite in fact.

"Are things...are you all right?" I asked suspiciously.

"Ye-es. I just need a wee-wee."

92

"I really don't want to know that. What did the letter say?"

"Nothing."

Mum must have heard us because she shouted from her room, "Err…Bella, into bed now, and Amber, get a move on."

"Bella," I hissed, "come on! Tell me!"

"Okay, okay. He told me to look at the moon tonight."

"WHAT?"

"Oh my gosh, are you deaf? He told me to look at the moon tonight!"

"What? Why?"

"Ambra! Don't make me get up!" Mum shouted. She only calls me Ambra when she's angry with me. It's kind of good because I know when I'm in trouble and can prepare myself. But kind of bad because when she calls me Ambra, I get scared.

Bella tried to whisper. She's not great at whispering. It's almost as loud as her normal voice, but at least she tried. "Because wherever Dad is in the world, he's staring up at the same moon as we are."

"THE MOON?"

"Amber, shh! Why are you shouting about the moon? Mum will think you've gone mad."

Hrrughhh!

"Think, Bella, think. Is that all he said? Nothing about your birthday party or anything?"

"Imagine if the moon was like a mirror, Amber! Then we'd be able to see him looking up and we could wave at him! That would be so cool!"

"Bella, please. Please. Try and remember. Didn't he say anything about your party? Or maybe about him not being a king and you getting the wrong idea?"

Bella looked at me like I was talking in Russian. "Amber, you're so nosy. If you want to talk to Dad, write your own letters."

We could hear Mum push back her squeaky chair and stomp across the floor of her bedroom toward us. I ran into my room and Bella dashed into the bathroom and locked the door.

That night, I thought about the moon and about Bella and about how impossible it seemed to sort this whole Dad mess out. I couldn't sleep for ages. The beast under my bed started snorting. I really didn't want him to wake up and get inside my mind because that would be it. So I thought of happy, dreamy things, like what apps I'd put on my new phone and which type of mechanical pencils I'd buy.

And then, for some strange reason, Locker Boy drifted into my mind. The whole boy thing was new to me. It was kind of confusing.

So I got out a pencil and some paper and started sketching Dream Dad again.

"Are you here?" I whispered to the drawing on the paper. Seriously, if anyone had seen me they'd have thought I was crazy.

"Of course," you said.

"Can I ask you something?"

"You can ask me anything."

When I finished drawing you, I propped myself up on my elbow and imagined that instead of being on paper, you were sitting on the end of my bed, reading.

"So there's this boy—"

"Here we go," you said, grinning and putting the book down.

"No, it's not like that. It's just that he makes me feel weird and *stupida* whenever I'm near him."

"Yeah," you said. "I know that feeling."

"But how can I tell if he likes me? Boys are weird. How do their minds work?"

"HAHAHAHAHA!" you said, laughing so much you nearly fell on the floor. "Try all your life and you will never, ever work that one out. Let me tell you how you can tell if a boy likes you. Ready?"

"Ready."

"Okay, so here goes:

1. He ignores you.
2. He says snappish things to you and walks away.
3. He makes fun of you.
4. He throws things at you and calls you names.
5. He slaps you on the arm and punches you whenever he gets the chance.

"Wow," I said, lifting my head to see if you were being serious. "How do you know all this stuff?"

"I watch *Life On Planet Boy*. You should watch it. You'll totally get why boys are so weird."

"Oh. So that's when they *like* you? But they do exactly those things when they DON'T like you! What's the difference?"

"There isn't one really. You can just tell. Sometimes, anyway."

I thought about that. It wasn't much help. But it was so cool to have someone to talk to about boys and how strange and unnatural they were.

FOURTeen-
QUATTORDICI-JŪ Shi

Fridays are usually a good thing. Fridays mean the weekend is coming. Friday is nearly-there-day.

But this one was just as horrible as any other day. Worse, even. It was the end of my first week at Spit Hill, and all I wanted to do was rewind and start the whole week again from the beginning.

I washed my face, got my hideous itchy uniform on, and tied up my hair. Chloe and her modern phone knew what time the bus was coming so I stomped in the rain to the bus stop to meet her. I had to get a new phone. I just had to. I wanted new art materials, but I *needed* a phone or I'd die of lack-of-technology disease. And without the bus app, I'd either have to go to school with Chloe every day for the rest of my life or stand waiting at the bus stop like a cavewoman. Not that they had buses in cavepeople times, but anyway.

Mrs. Venables from downstairs smiled and waved as she went the other way in her lime-green car. She was a bit scary because she shouted in a shrieky voice at her children and always looked like she was just about to flip out and start screaming, but I smiled and waved back because by then I was thinking about a job. How could I earn money? I had fifty pounds. If I had sixty more I could get a Jupiter, which is, like, the coolest phone you have EVER seen in your ENTIRE life. Apart from an iPhone, but that costs zillions. And a few really expensive others that have *sugoi* ("great" in Japanese) art apps on them and styluses and things that make my mouth water. Why did life have to be so expensive?

Maybe I could do stuff for the Venables family, like help their kids with their homework or set the table because Mrs. Venables comes home so late. Mr. Venables was usually home but he was always watching soccer and quiz shows on TV. I could hear the clapping through the floor. No wonder Mrs. Venables looked like she was about to flip all the time because that would drive me nuts as well.

99

Chloe was at the bus stop waving at me to hurry up. She was standing with two other girls who I recognized from our sixth-grade assembly. Obviously, by the end of day one, Chloe had made friends with everyone in sight and added everyone's number to her iPhone, which her dad gave her when he got an upgrade. The two girls she was standing with, Eva and Millie, lived nearby too, so Chloe had arranged for us all to go to school together. They were all chatting about Justin Bieber and showing photos of their dogs and summer breaks on their phones. I hated Justin Bieber. I didn't have a dog. And we didn't go on vacation.

"Haven't you got any photos, Amber?" Millie asked.

"Um…my phone hasn't got a camera."

"Oh." Millie looked surprised. "No offense or anything, but it's a bit like a granny phone."

"Yeah. Just call me Cavegirl."

She smiled at me with pity and confusion and went back to the conversation, so I just stared out of the window and in my head, I drew the world as it should be.

For a while it made me feel better.

But then I got to school.

100

I got in trouble in math and French for not doing my home- work but they didn't give me 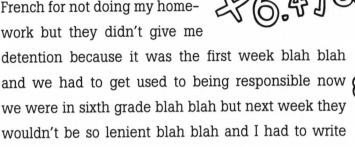 detention because it was the first week blah blah and we had to get used to being responsible now we were in sixth grade blah blah but next week they wouldn't be so lenient blah blah and I had to write everything down in my homework diary blah blah. *Yes, yes, whatever*, I thought, *please shut up and leave me alone*.

Then, as I stomped grumpily to the cafeteria at lunchtime, I saw her. Joanne Pyke stood at the other end of the corridor with two of her friends. I ducked but it was too late. She said something to them. Their movements became jerky, excited, and edgy, and they started moving quickly toward me.

Panic flooded through me and I froze.

Chloe, Eva, and Millie were walking ten steps ahead of me, chatting. I started walking faster to catch up with them because I realized that being frozen is not the best way to escape from dangerous people. I had friends. They'd stand up for me, surely. They'd all jump to help me out.

"Oy! Oy, you! Tiny!" Joanne yelled as she got closer to me. I ducked and carried on scurrying away. "You're the one who beat up my little brother!"

I wanted to shout back at her, "I didn't beat him up, I just twisted his arm, and the idiot deserved it!" but it really wasn't the best time.

I heard them break into a run so I started running too. I pushed past Chloe, Eva, and Millie and sprinted past the lockers, trying to get to the double doors that led to the playground.

"Amber!" Chloe shouted. "What are you—?"

As Joanne and her sidekicks got closer, I was sure my friends would see what was happening and block the way, or scream, "Hey! Back off!" and then Joanne would see I had an army of fearless friends and leave me alone. Why wasn't that happening? Why?

I turned to look.

My so-called friends had all moved out of the way so Joanne and her sidekicks could get to me quicker.

Joanne's friend grabbed my arm before I made it to the double doors and in a second all three of them were grabbing at me. Joanne was snarling, "I'll teach you not to touch my brother, you midget!"

They pulled and tugged me across the corridor, away from the doors.

And then I saw it.

The big, sticky, smelly trash bin at the end of the row of lockers. I was going into a disease-ridden bacterial grime pot of dust and gum and food wrappers! No! NOOOOO!!!

My body went rigid. They held me tighter and a giant spasm of shock and dread jolted through me, making me roar and yelp. Which probably came out as a gerbil squeak.

With each thump of my blood in my head more horror flashed into my brain. Sticky. Dirty. Stinky. GOO. YUCKY. GERMS.

No!!

There was no way was I going in that bin!

I had to stop them. I started struggling madly but it was like they were holding me with claws of steel. They dragged me closer, and in no time I was right beside the big bin and I knew they were about to slam me in like a basketball into a net when a screech came from the other end of the corridor.

103

"Joanne Pyke, what on *earth* is going on in here? Put Amber down this second!"

It was none other than Miss Figgis. I didn't think I'd ever—EVER—be happy to see her but believe me, right then, I was delighted. And because her voice was so loud and high and shocking they just froze and dropped me on to the floor. Which was also pretty humiliating but nothing compared to the bin.

"Joanne! What are you doing? What happened to all those breathing techniques I taught you? Go to Mrs. Hill RIGHT NOW! All three of you!"

The girls glared at her and turned to growl at me, but to my utter relief, they picked up their bags and slouched off to the principal's office, mumbling.

I think I only started breathing again at that moment. I stood up and brushed the dust off myself. I hate dust. It's basically diseased bits of fur mixed with infected fluff, ant poo, and flakes of dead skin.

"Are you all right, Amber?" Miss Figgis asked.

"Yeah, I'm fine." I wasn't exactly fine but what was I supposed to say?

"Can you come over here for second?"

I felt a sea of eyes on me as Miss Figgis took me

toward the doors I had been trying to get out of. They were to one side so at least we weren't in full view of the cafeteria. Those double doors were still pretty tempting. I could have just bolted out, found a way over the fence, and run home. And never come back ever again.

"We're going to talk about this in our session on Tuesday," Miss Figgis said, firmly.

"Oh no, please. I really don't want to talk about this when that girl Joanne is in the room."

"Oh? Well, then we'll talk about it now," she said. "Come with me."

I rolled my eyes and picked up my bag.

We walked to the staff room and she excused me from the next class, which was history, so that was one small bonus.

"You do need to eat something. Do you want me to come with you to the cafeteria?"

As if.

"Um...it's okay. I have a sandwich in my bag."

"Good, so meet me next period in room six in the Humanities building."

I nodded slowly and stumbled off.

*

I felt like Katniss in the arena in *The Hunger Games*. Bloodthirsty eyes followed my every move. I kept my head down. I really didn't want to go back to my so-called friends but Chloe was running toward me down the corridor nearly wetting herself with the excitement of it all.

"Why is that girl after you?" she asked. "The one who looks like a wrestler."

I really didn't want to go into it. "Oh, it's just a big mistake," I said. Which it was.

I couldn't exactly blame them for not standing up for me. They barely knew me. I didn't even speak to them on the bus. And Joanne Pyke had big muscley arms that could have thrown for gold in the Olympic shotput.

After lunch, I wandered around the Humanities building for ages until I found room six and went in. Miss Figgis was already there. She was dressed from head to toe in green, which I hadn't noticed when I was lying on the floor in the corridor. My attention must have been somewhere else.

"Come and sit here, Amber," she said.

I felt tears stinging my eyes as I went to the

106

chair, but I really didn't want her to see them. I didn't feel like telling her anything because trash-bin germs had been *this close* to touching me and I felt massively humiliated, but I felt I owed her. If it wasn't for her I'd be stuffed in that filthy grime pit right now.

"What's happened between you and Joanne?" she asked as I sat down. "Why is she bullying you? You've only been at Spit Hill for a week."

"She's not bullying me," I muttered. "She just wants to dump me in the bin."

Miss Figgis looked at me as if I was a total moron. "What do you think bullying is, Amber?"

"I know what it is. It's when someone, like, picks on you and won't leave you alone and wants to hurt you or take money from you and stuff."

"Don't you think Joanne is picking on you? Doesn't she want to hurt you? Make fun of you? I think you'll find that kind of behavior is called bullying."

She had a point. But she didn't know what I'd done to Joanne's little brother.

"It's not really bullying. Arm twisting's not bullying and neither is bin dumping. Not really."

"I think you might need to explain this from the beginning," she said, tying back her brown, curly hair.

So I did. Even though I knew it was a bad idea.

After I finished, Miss Figgis sighed. "What a big old mix-up!" she said. "Well, you have to promise me something now, young Amber. You have to tell me if Joanne ever does this again, okay?"

Like I was going to do that. I smiled, which isn't technically a promise, and kind of nodded, which isn't one either.

"Good. So I'll see you on Tuesday at the Inward Reach class, okay? I'm looking forward to seeing your drawing."

Gulp.

Miss Figgis stood up and smiled kindly. "Say no to bullies, Amber."

Right. I imagined, just for a second, walking over to Joanne Pyke and saying "No!" to her in a don't-mess-with-me-voice. She was hardly going to say, "Oh, okay then," and walk away.

I mean, really.

"Are you all right?" Miss Figgis asked.

"I'm fine. And thanks, Miss Figgis. You saved me."

She grinned. "Pay me back by drawing a fabulous picture, okay?"

I gave her an eeky half-smile and watched her walk out.

FifTeen-
QUINDICI-JŪ GO

When I got home, I went straight to my room and lay on my bed with my face in the pillow.

Mum was cooking. I could smell onions frying. But it wasn't long before she came and knocked on my door.

I didn't answer. I couldn't. I was so shocked and distressed that my lips were kind of jammed together.

Mum asked through the door, "Amber? What are you doing in there? Is everything okay?"

I didn't answer so she opened my bedroom door, even though it has a sign on it saying:

DO NOT
COME IN
EVER!

"You've still got your shoes and coat on," she said. "Your first week was that good, huh?"

She walked over and sat on the edge of my bed. She rubbed my back, and for a second I really wanted to tell her all about it. I wanted to pour my heart out and cry and wail like a five-year-old and tell her it wasn't fair, but I just couldn't.

"It'll get better, Amber. It's not easy starting a new school. You'll meet new friends and you'll settle down. It'll be fine."

I swallowed and tried not to cry. Of course it wasn't going to be fine.

"Come out soon and eat. I'm cooking some...oh, shoot—"

And she ran to get the onions off the stove.

Mum made me do my homework at the kitchen table instead of in my room. I think she was worried about me and wanted to cheer me up but I wasn't in the mood. I sat at the table but I couldn't concentrate. It was partly because I was still in bin shock and partly because Mum and Bella were talking about Bella's party.

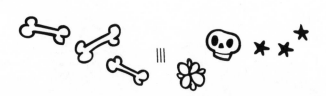

It was in a week. Bella was inviting twenty six-year-old kids and the party was going to be at our house. Those three things already made me *molto* nervous.

I didn't have a lock on my door. All I could think of were twenty sticky-fingered hurricanes ripping through all my stuff, touching everything with their filthy, snotty, germy hands. For someone with dirt phobia like me, that was a huge problem.

To make it worse, Bella said, "Mummy, I really really want Clopsie the Clown! Can I have Clopsie? Please, Mummy?"

I groaned.

Clopsie the Clown was this stupid entertainer. She did exactly the same routine, word for word, at every kids' party so everyone—the kids, the parents, the babies in buggies—knew it by heart. It was no surprise at all when Clopsie made the birthday girl's badge disappear and then reappear on the fluffy bunny under the hat—everyone was waiting for her to say, "Where's Katie's birthday ribbon?" They'd all yell, "Under the hat!" and she'd shout, "It can't be under this hat, can it? There's nothing under this hat!"

Then they'd all screech when they saw the ribbon on the "surprise" bunny and sing Katie the birthday bunny song.

It was so stupid.

"Bella, you've seen that routine about fifty times!" I said. "Do something different. Everyone gets Clopsie to do their parties."

"But I want Clopsie to sing to *me*!"

Mum put the rice on the stove and went to call Clopsie to see if she was free. "It's highly unlikely though, Bella," Mum said as she googled Clopsie's number. "She's bound to be booked up at such short notice. But there's no harm in trying."

Mum called the number and started chatting and shrieking and laughing with Clopsie even though she didn't even know her. It was like they were best friends. It wasn't surprising because Mum can really talk. She has long chats with shopkeepers and knows all the neighbors for miles around. She talks to old ladies in the supermarket and tells random strangers in clothes shops whether or not they should buy whatever is it they're trying on and why. And at parents' night she chats to all my teachers about things that have nothing to do with me or my education and sends them links to websites she thinks they'll like. She's so embarrassing.

So while Mum was talking to her new friend Clopsie, Bella was sitting next to her saying again and again, "Can she come, Mummy? Can she?"

I gave up on my homework, took out a piece of paper, and started drawing Bella's party as it really needed to be.

I don't know how much time passed but suddenly I smelled burning. I looked in the kitchen at the pot of rice, and there was smoke coming out of it.

"MUM!" I yelled.

"Just a minute, Amber, I'm still on the phone," she said. And she carried on chatting. Then, just as I shouted, "Mum! The rice! It's on fire!" the smoke alarm went off, making a really evil noise.

I heard Mum yell, "I have to go!" and she threw the phone on the table and ran through the smoke into the kitchen. She turned off the gas, stuck a dish towel under the faucet, and started yelling, "Girls! Girls, are you okay?" to make sure we weren't dead or something. Which we weren't, obviously, but

114

one more minute and we might have been. She threw the wet towel over the smouldering pan and opened the window to get the smoke out. The kitchen stank and the alarm was screaming. Bella and I had no idea what to do so we stood staring in shock at the mayhem.

Mum grabbed a chair, stood on it, and pulled the smoke alarm off the ceiling but she had to rip the battery out because she didn't know how else to turn it off. IT WAS SO LOUD! Once it was off, I heard knocking on our door so I ran to get it.

It was Pete from upstairs.

"Shall I call the fire department?" he asked. His eyes were wide with fear and he was panting from running down the stairs.

The last time Mum burnt something, which wasn't very long ago, Mrs. Venables called 911 and we had sirens screaming outside and firemen running up the stairs with their hoses.

"No, it's fine, thanks, Pete. No flames this time."

He said, "Well, if you're sure. I don't feel like being burned alive this evening."

I smiled but it was so embarrassing. I don't know

how many times my mum's left something on the stove or in the oven and forgotten about it but the firemen know her by name now. There's one fire-man called Mick who we see sometimes in the super-market and he shouts out, "Hi, Bob! Hope you're not buying any raw ingredients! You stay away from that stove now, you hear?" and then he cracks up.

Mum blushes and says, "Tsk, I'm not that bad!"

But it's not true. She is. Pete and Mrs. Venables keep all the fridge magnets and leaflets for fast food delivery that come through the front door. They give them to my mum to drop the hint that she should leave cooking to people who won't kill their neigh-bors every time they make lasagna.

Now when Mum is cooking, Bella and I leave our sneakers on so if we need to run out of the house in a hurry, we're ready. I seriously hope we don't inherit the bad cook gene from my mum. Or her fashion sense. Or her loud laugh. Or her craving to talk to random stran-gers all the time. Imagine what weird genes we've got from her that are lurking undiscovered under our skin. And what about the ones from my dad?

Maybe I got this phobia about dirt from him. Maybe

he hates celery and gave that to me. Does he have a birthmark on his arm, there, underneath, on the soft bit, like me? Would he get nervous about loads of six-year-old kids coming to his house?

I guess he wouldn't know that, seeing as he shipped out and left.

After I shut the door, I sighed and went back into the kitchen. Bella was grinning and sniggering because she loves drama and craziness and I'm sure she'd have said, "Mum, do it again! Burn something else!" if it wasn't for the fact that my mum was in tears by then.

"Mum?" I asked. "Why are you crying?"

I kind of wish I hadn't asked because then she started sobbing and saying she was trying her best and she didn't know what else she could do but her best but sometimes it was just too much and she couldn't do it all on her own. I wasn't really sure what she was talking about because it was only burnt rice and we didn't even like her rice—it was always really gloopy or tasted like a bonfire.

"Mummy?" Bella asked. "Are you crying because Clopsie can't come to my party?"

117

"Oh, Bella, no," Mum said, wiping her eyes. "I didn't even tell you! Clopsie CAN come! She's had a cancellation."

Bella started jumping around screaming while Mum flapped her hands through the smoky kitchen. Then she went out on the balcony to calm down, and when she came back in she ordered us pizza from Slice (which was fine by me). But after the pizza she started crying again so it obviously wasn't just about burning dinner.

Bella sat beside her telling her not to worry because we'd look after her but then she cried even more because, she said, *she* was supposed to be the one saying that stuff to *us*.

Parents are so confusing. Maybe two are even worse than one. Maybe dads are just as complicated and we're better off without one, I don't know. What I did know was that if I'd told her all *my* problems as well, it would have made it much, much worse.

When I went to bed that night I lay there thinking. Bella was still expecting Dad to come to her party.

Seriously, what did she think would happen if Dad really did turn up?

My mum would be so shocked.

Nonna would probably hit him over the head with a frying pan.

I would get in a massive sulk. Or storm off.

It was a good thing he wasn't coming because it would ruin the party.

I needed to talk to someone about all my disasters. But no one would understand the whole range and variety of problems I had. No one would get how weirded out I felt about showing people my artwork for the competition. Nonna wouldn't get the school stuff. My so-called school friends wouldn't get the whole history about my dad, and I wasn't about to tell them. My friends from my old elementary school were never that close anyway so I wasn't about to call them up and explain all my nightmares. They'd say, "Err...ooo-kay. Why are you telling *me*?"

And I couldn't tell Mum. No way. Not about the letters I'd written to Bella pretending to be my dad. And not about Joanne Pyke. She'd freak out. Big-time.

There was no one in the whole world who would

understand each of the catastrophes of my life and still be on my side.

But then I remembered.

There was one person who would get it.

Just one.

sixteen-
sedici-jū roku

"Are you here?" I asked my empty room. Good thing no one was standing outside my door listening.

This time I didn't get out my pencils and draw you first. I was checking to see if you could be around straight away. Because what if I was out and had no paper? What then?

"Course I am," you said. You sat on the end of my bed, playing with your toes through your socks. You were wearing all black, like a ninja. Apart from the socks, which had red-and-white stripes and looked more like *Cat in the Hat* socks than ninja socks.

I sighed. It must have been a huge sigh because you said, "Jeez, you'd better sit down and tell me what's up."

So I let it all out.

I told you that the letter I'd written back to Bella hadn't worked and she still thought Dad was coming to her party.

"Write her another one," you said. "And keep writing them until she gets it."

I nodded. But Bella and her letters were not my only problem.

I told you about what had happened with Joanne that day and about Miss Figgis and the art competition.

"I want to change schools," I said. "And I've only been there a week. Or go back to elementary school where everything was easy."

"Really? You want to go back in there with all the five-year-olds?"

I made a face. I didn't really. But it was better than going back to Spit Hill on Monday morning.

"I haven't made any real friends yet," I said.

"You've only been there a week! Give it time. Just chillax and be yourself. Everyone will love you once they get to know you."

It was easy enough to say but how could I be myself when I wasn't even sure who I was meant to be?

"Do you know how weird it is to be half Japanese and half Italian? It's messed up," I said.

"Yeah, you're all mixed up like a salad. Salad Girl is a good name. How about Salad Girl instead of all those names you hate?"

"This isn't about my name. I'll show you what the problem is."

I went to my desk and came back with a small mirror from Claire's that Nonna gave me. I held it up.

"Look," I said.

You looked. "I know. I'm so handsome," you said.

"No, look at *me*."

"What am I supposed to be looking at?"

"Look at my face. Look how my eyes go up in the corners. Look at my feathery eyebrows and how dark and straight my hair is. When I look in the mirror, there's this Japanese-looking person staring back at me. But when I look around at people in my family, in my street, in my school, none of them have those things. My family are all Italians. Which is great and everything, but we don't look even remotely related. And none of them knows anything about Japan."

"So?"

123

"So I have no *homies*."

"Homies?"

"I know that loads of people are half this and half that: I'm not the only one. But still. I don't speak Japanese. I know nothing about Japan unless I google it. I can count to ten but so can anyone who does karate. I just look Japanese and have Japanese bits in my body. I don't know one single Japanese person now my dad has left. Apart from Bella and she doesn't count. I feel like an alien. Like I'm pretending to be Japanese but it's all a big lie."

You looked at me and smiled. "I can be Japanese if you like."

In a second, you transformed into a sumo wrestler. It was a good thing I hadn't drawn you first because I don't even know how to draw someone that shape. You were hugely fat, with long tied-up hair and weird, small underpants that showed a bit too much of your wobbly butt.

"Please. Way too much flesh. And it doesn't help me much."

"Oh. Sorry." You put on a robe but you stayed like that. I think you liked it.

There was a knock at my bedroom door. I jumped because I wasn't expecting it at all.

"Amber?"

It was my mum.

"You'd better disappear," I said to you. So you did. Even though you weighed as much as a pregnant elephant, you just went *paff* and you were gone.

Mum opened the door and looked in. "Amber? Who are you talking to?"

"Um...no one. I was just doing... I was just talking to myself," I said.

"Amber, please tell me what's going on," Mum said, coming in. "I'm really worried about you."

I didn't want my mum to have more stuff to worry about than she had already. She looked all sad and frowny.

So I decided to tell her.

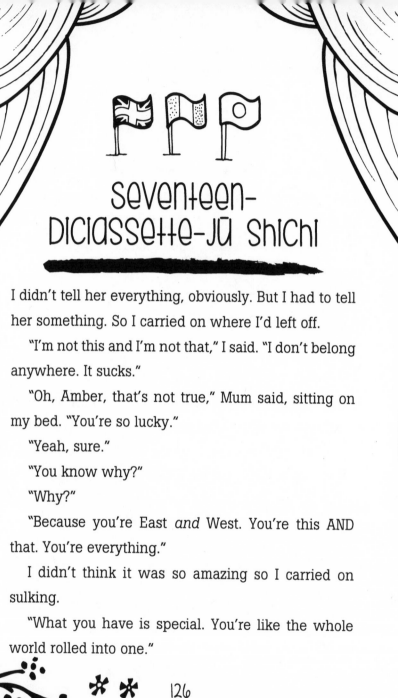

seventeen- DICIasSette-JŪ ShICHI

I didn't tell her everything, obviously. But I had to tell her something. So I carried on where I'd left off.

"I'm not this and I'm not that," I said. "I don't belong anywhere. It sucks."

"Oh, Amber, that's not true," Mum said, sitting on my bed. "You're so lucky."

"Yeah, sure."

"You know why?"

"Why?"

"Because you're East *and* West. You're this AND that. You're everything."

I didn't think it was so amazing so I carried on sulking.

"What you have is special. You're like the whole world rolled into one."

"Great."

"It *is* great, actually. When you get older you'll realize how awesome that is."

But I didn't want to realize it when I was older. I wanted to understand it now. Since my dad had left, the Japanese half of me was missing, and I wanted to feel whole. I wanted a mum *and* a dad. And I wanted to feel like I belonged somewhere.

"When you look around you, what do you see, Amber? Not in your room. I mean outside."

"Houses? Graffiti?"

"Think bigger than that."

"I dunno. Buses? Shops? Trees?"

"Let me put it this way. You're going to inherit something extraordinary, Amber. Do you know that?"

Ooh. Inherit. I was suddenly interested. What was I going to inherit? Was there a room full of gold somewhere, like Harry Potter's parents left him in Gringotts? Was it a mansion by the sea? A trillion pounds in cash? Some huge cell phone company so I could take my pick of a different phone every day? An amazing samurai sword from my great-grandfather?

"So what is it?" I asked. "What am I going to inherit? Is it, like, some family fortune?"

Mum looked at me and raised that eyebrow. "Not exactly. It's nothing material. But that doesn't mean it isn't valuable, because it's priceless."

I was so confused. "What do you mean?"

"We might not be wealthy, Amber, but that doesn't mean we didn't give you something."

"Ooo-kay. So what is it?"

Mum smiled. "We gave you the whole world. This amazing, beautiful planet. It's so much bigger than what you've seen until now. It's vast and it's breathtaking. It's the most priceless thing there is, better than any family fortune. *That* is your inheritance. It's all yours."

I didn't mean to look disappointed but it didn't seem so great after a room full of gold or a house by the sea.

Mum must have noticed my lip curling because she said, "I know that doesn't seem so special when everyone else has been given the same present as you. But it means something, Amber."

I looked at her. I had no idea what it meant. I

think she realized that so she just went ahead and told me.

"It means that you might not be from just one place where they speak just one language, but that really doesn't matter. It's actually an advantage. There's a big, beautiful world out there and it's getting smaller and more interconnected every day. Don't feel like you don't belong anywhere because it's just not true. The whole world is yours. You belong everywhere."

I smiled. I have to admit, that made me feel a teeny bit better.

"Besides," Mum said quietly, "your dad did give you something before he left. You know that, don't you?"

I wasn't sure I even wanted it. Whatever it was. But I was still curious.

"He *gave* me something? What was it?"

"Guess."

"I dunno. A diamond ring?"

"Nope."

"The keys to a Porsche on my eighteenth birthday?"

"Uh-uh."

"A shop full of art supplies and a new phone?

"Better."

"Better than a new phone? What is it?"

Mum smiled. "He gave you his love, Amber. Oceans of it. Really."

I didn't say anything. The black hole in me felt heavier than ever, sucking the air out of my lungs like a vacuum cleaner.

"It doesn't feel like that," I whispered. "It feels like he left me with oceans of nothing at all."

"I know. But it's not true. He loved you."

She tried to give me a hug, but right then I didn't want one. I just needed to be alone for a while so I buried my head in my pillow again.

Sometimes you have to wait a long time to understand things. I think this was one of those things. I think if I ever understand it, it'll be a long time from now.

Eighteen-
DICIOTTO-JŪ Hachi

On Saturday morning, Bella handed me another letter.

Dier Dad.

Are you comming to my party in a limoozine or a helicokter? I'm so hapy coz Colpse the Cown is comming to. And Nonna sed she will buy me new partie shues. Lelo ones.

Love Bella

P.S. Does a red shurt go with green trosis? Amber said it looks wird. But Amber is not the most fashunabulist person. She dosent even war heir clips

It made me mad. She just wasn't listening!

And what do I know about red shirts and green trousers? It DOES look weird.

I couldn't think about it. I didn't want to think about it. Not about Bella and not about my dad. I had to focus on what I needed, and what I needed was money so I could get a phone. Mum was supposed to be giving us allowance money but she always forgot. I had to find another way.

We were having breakfast in our pajamas. It's, like, a tradition in our house on Saturday mornings. Even my mum does it. We don't get dressed until we have to, and sometimes we stay in our pajamas all day. Or at least until Nonna comes over and shouts, "*Andatevi a vestire!*" at us so we all have to go and get dressed.

Mum sat cross-legged on the chair in her blue checked pajama pants and a big orange cardigan. Her hair looked like the scribbles that Bella used to draw on the walls with red crayons. She was eating toast and reading a biography about some famous musician. Bella was making a face on her plate

by dribbling yogurt on to it with a spoon. It was quite good and quite gross at the same time.

I was fiddling with the jelly lid deciding when it was a good time to bring up what was on my mind. I was on a mission. I needed a new phone. No more messing around.

So I just went for it.

"Mum," I asked, "what can I do to earn money?"

"Hmm?" she said, looking up from the book.

I had to say it again.

"What do you need money for?"

"Stuff."

"Well, you do need some new pencils. And I can't afford to keep buying that special paper you like. Wait—this isn't about a phone, is it? Because you need art materials more than you need a phone."

"Mum," I said. "What do you take me for? Don't be silly."

She looked at me suspiciously. She knew it was for a phone—I could just tell.

"Well," she said, pushing the book to one side, "you can do some chores around here and help me out. Actually...I don't think I should pay you for helping out in your own home—I think you should do it for free because we *all* live here and we *all* want to live in a nice place. And don't roll your eyes at me, Ambra Miyamoto."

"Mum?"

"Mmm?"

"What can I do to earn money from someone else? Someone that might have cash on them more regularly?"

Mum laughed. "Yeah, that's probably a better idea. Well, you could...wash cars?"

"Apart from that."

"Um...how about dog walking?"

"I'd have to pick up poop. And smell their stinky dog breath."

"Of course. What about helping Mandi next door? She's got her hands full with the twins—they're not even two yet and now she's got the baby. You could help her at teatimes."

"No thanks. Her twins are all sticky and mucky and she might make me change the baby's diaper."

"Amber, if you're going to be this picky—"

"Can't you ask if anyone needs, like, small jobs done?"

Mum looked out of the window, which she always does when she's thinking about something. Maybe the answer is written on the clouds or something. Maybe I should try it.

"I don't see why not," she said. "Good idea. I'll ask around."

I imagined going to Mrs. Beadle's place two doors down and tidying the bookshelves or pumping up Pete's bike tires on a Sunday morning. I could read to the Venables kids or help them with their spelling. I was forced to do it anyway with Bella for free. Mind you, Bella's spelling really needed all the help it could get.

I finished breakfast and went to my room. I spent the next three hours drawing. It wasn't for the art competition though. I was transforming my bedroom into my ideal space. The glass ceiling would be made of special glass so it didn't get too hot in the summer, but it would let in enough light and give me a full 360-degree view of thunderstorms and stars. It would have a telescope, obviously, and a fridge and a cupboard full of snacks and a big, big bed and a bouncy trampoline floor.

I don't know how much time passed but suddenly Mum knocked at the door.

"Come in."

She was dressed and her hair was pulled back in a clip. Nonna must have arrived.

"Guess what? I found you a job," Mum said.

"Great! What is it?"

"Do you want the good news or the bad news?"

I paused. How could a job have good news or bad news attached to it? I was confused.

"Um—"

"The good news is, you're going to be paid well. Five pounds an hour. That's good money, Amber."

I looked at her suspiciously. "Go...on."

"The bad news is, it's for Nonna."

"Why is that bad news?"

Mum was scrunching up her face like she couldn't tell me.

"Mum, what?"

"You're not going to like it."

"Tell me."

"You have to clean out her cat litter trays. You'd be doing us all a favor—those litter trays stink."

136

Eek. There was no way. I mean, this was me we were talking about.

Did I want a phone that badly?

"Hasn't anything else come up? Like watering flowers while someone's away?"

"Not yet. That's it. Take it or leave it."

Cat litter trays. *Blurcch.* I felt sick just thinking of it. I just couldn't. I'd die. It was worse than cars and diapers and dog poo put together. I sighed and shook my head.

"Can I tell you in five minutes?"

"Take as long as you like."

She went out and closed the door.

You were sitting in a rocking chair, smoking a pipe. Like a wise owl of a father who was really good at giving advice. Which was just what I needed.

"Good afternoon. Everything all right?" you asked.

"Nnnugh. Bad news."

"Did war break out?"

"No."

"Did United lose the cup?"

"How should I know?"

137

"What's the bad news then?"

"I got a job."

"Oh, that's terrible. Tragic. A catastrophe. I feel awful for you. That's a major world disaster."

"You haven't heard what it is yet."

"So tell me."

"Cleaning out Nonna's cat litter trays."

"Uch. Gross!"

"Exactly."

I sat on the floor. You carried on rocking and puffing on your pipe. We were quiet for a bit, thinking about just how revolting that job was and just how desperate you would need to be in order to agree to it.

"Do you need the money that badly?" you asked.

"Obviously, or we wouldn't be having this conversation."

You looked at me. "So...?"

"But it's disgusting. I have a problem with dirt and muck and particularly poo. Why does it have to be that, of all things? Why?"

"Look," you said, "you either need that money or you don't. What do you want it for?"

"I have to get a proper phone."

"You certainly do!" you said. "You can't walk around with that pathetic, embarrassing lump of plastic a second longer. You need some decent technology in your life. But isn't there any other job going? Why litter trays?"

"That's all there is. I'm not even twelve yet—it's not like I can just get a job anywhere."

"So…you don't have any choice, is that what you're saying?"

"Basically."

You looked at me as though the answer was obvious.

I sighed. "Yeah, you're right."

I went back out to Mum. Nonna had fallen asleep on the sofa while she was reading the paper and Mum was doing the shopping list for the party with Bella.

"I'll do it," I said.

"Do what?" Mum asked, not looking up.

"The job. At Nonna's."

Mum's eyes nearly popped out and her mouth opened wide like a goldfish swallowing a blue whale. "Wow, you really want this money, don't you?"

"Yes," I said. "Yes, I do. When do I start?"

Nineteen-
Diciannove-jū ku

I started that afternoon, which was a bit *rapido* for my liking but I didn't want to waste any time. There was no way I was going to school every day with Chloe Cain and all those girls with cameras and Instagram. I felt like a total loser.

I packed a bag of things I would need, then Nonna walked me back to her place. She lives about twenty minutes' walk away.

When we got to Nonna's house I sat in her kitchen for ages, trying to find the courage to start. Nonna fed me pasta and then lemon cake so the courage took quite a long time to come. But after about half an hour, Nonna said, "*Andiamo.*" Which means "Let's go."

I felt ill. But I gritted my teeth and followed her.

Nonna's house was really nice and everything: it was colorful and had fat cushions everywhere and there was always good food to eat, unlike at my house. But she had this conservatory and that was home to her disgusting cats. Trust me, it was a room I never went into when I went to visit her. As soon as you got near it, you could smell the cat pee. It was like acid.

When she opened the conservatory door the smell hit me with full force. My nostril skin started dissolving. My stomach buckled.

I was about to change my mind and run but then I remembered the money. *You can do this, Amber*, I told myself. *You will not die. Humans do not die from cat pee. You can do this.*

Then I wondered if anyone *had* ever died of cat pee but I couldn't google it at home because I was banned from the computer. Of course, I could have checked it there and then on my phone if I had a phone with Internet. Which just proved it to me. I was endangering my life walking around with that cavegirl phone. It was DANGEROUS.

Nonna's disgusting cats followed me, meowing.

All I could imagine was them being full of fleas and diseases and licking themselves with cat-food flavor furball tongues.

"*Ti faccio vedere io,*" Nonna said, but I looked at her like I didn't understand so she sighed and switched to English. "I show you where isss everyting and you can start the work, no?"

She showed me where she kept the kitty litter behind the door, and then she showed me the litter trays.

There were two of them. They were sitting on the floor near the window. They were gray and stinking and covered with lumps of brown (and I knew exactly what that was). I looked at the sludgy grit caked in this gray dust and there were thick clumps of wet from the pee. I thought I would die right there on the floor and maybe even be the first person ever to actually die from cat pee. But then I told myself it was better to stay alive for a bit longer and die somewhere less smelly.

"*Va tutto bene,* Ambra?" Nonna asked. "Are you okay? You look liddle bit green."

I nodded but I didn't want to talk because then I

wouldn't be able to block my nose from the inside and I was worried about fainting.

"I juss leave you, *si*?"

I nodded.

Nonna went out. I'm sure she was grinning.

I looked at the litter trays.

My stomach lurched.

You can do this, Amber, I told myself.

So I got ready. I unpacked my bag and set it all out on the floor. Then I mixed the disinfectant solution in a small bucket with some water. I took out the latex gloves and put on five pairs, one on top of the other. Then I put on Mum's rainproof plastic jacket, pulled the sleeves down over the gloves and closed them with strong elastic bands so nothing would escape up my arms. Then I took out my nose clip for swimming and diving, and placed it over my nose. Last of all, I got the black bags ready.

I looked at the trays. I wanted to cry.

This was the worst day of my life. Even worse than nearly being thrown in the trash bin or being bitten by a dog when I was six.

But I thought about being able to buy my own

phone. I would finally be cool and not dinosaurish. I'd have my own camera and my own photos on my own brand-new gadget. I could download my own apps. I'd have my own bus schedule and I wouldn't have to rely on Chloe anymore. I'd be able to post pictures of random stuff on Instagram. I'd be able to google cat pee death whenever I needed to. I'd be part of the modern world.

It wasn't going to solve *all* the other problems in my life but it was a good start.

I started scraping all that gross wet lumpy stuff out of the litter trays with a dustpan and plopping it into the black bag.

I won't tell you how disgusting it was. Or how many times I thought I'd puke. Or how freaked out I was about the germs and the diseases and the death I was obviously exposing myself to. I'm sure I went green and white and blue, that's for sure. Like the national flag of Vomitland. But I did what I was being paid to do as quickly as I could, and then I got out of there.

I put the disgusting germy gloves in three lots of

plastic bags and into the black bag, said good-bye to Nonna (who was really happy with my work) and took the black bag to the wheelie bin outside. Then I went home and spent the rest of the day washing my hands up to the elbow and rinsing my germ-exposed mouth out with mouthwash.

I took the five pounds Nonna gave me and put it in my drawer.

Just fifty-five pounds to go. That meant I had to work at Nonna's eleven more times.

Eughh.

TWENTY-VENTI-NI JŪ

Doing my homework took ages because I spent most of Sunday staring out of the window, dreading Monday, when I'd have to go back to school.

Miss Figgis's class had been bad enough before, but now I had Joanne Pyke and the art competition to deal with.

I imagined doing all kinds of things to get out of it.

I could pretend I was sick and go to the office. I didn't know what Spit Hill was like, but at Parker Harris you had to be bleeding to death before they called your parents.

I could pretend I'd forgotten about the Inward Reach class but Miss Figgis would probably come looking for me.

I thought of skipping school completely but I knew my mum would go mad if she found out, and anyway, I didn't have anywhere to go. Mum worked from home most days and I didn't want to hang around on the streets.

I had no choice.

Joanne would catch up with me at some stage, and I could feel that day creeping closer. I could feel the germs on the inside of those bins waiting to stick on to me the minute I was slammed in.

I needed to get some air, so I went out of my room to give Bella the reply to her latest letter.

Dear Bella,

I'm not coming in a helicopter or in a limousine because I AM NOT COMING. Seriously, are you deaf? And the color is YELLOW, not lelo. But I hope you enjoy your party. Which by the way would be much more interesting and fun if it didn't have some boring and annoying entertainer like

Clopsie the Clown. Just saying.

Love, **DAD**

If she didn't get it this time, I really couldn't see what else I could do.

But later that afternoon, when I was practicing my *kata* in the sitting room, Bella made sure Mum was in the kitchen and then handed me a letter.

"Another one?" I asked.

"Yep."

"Don't you think it's getting a bit much?"

"Dad likes it. He told me."

I squinted at her. "You sure about that? I think he's getting really irritated, actually."

"Just mail it, okay?"

I had to take it to my room because I couldn't hide it up my shirt and do karate *katas*. When I got in there, I opened it.

> Dier Dad,
> Shall I marriy Ben Harper? He's 7. Is that to old for me?
>   Love, Bella

Marry? Ben Harper??

Bella was crazy.

I grabbed a pen and some clean paper and wrote back. I couldn't give it to her for a couple of days but at least it was done.

> Dear Bella,
>
> You have a bit of time to think about that. Maybe, like, twenty years or something. If you still like Ben Harper when you're twenty-six then fine but you should know that his big sister is totally obsessed with Justin Bieber. You might not want to marry into a family like that.
>
>   Love, DAD

Twenty-one-
Ventuno-NI JŪ IChl

In the morning, Bella was her usual self. She was humming at breakfast and making another cheesy bracelet.

I had to get out of there.

I wanted to get an early bus and avoid Chloe so I waited at the bus stop like a cavewoman. I wasn't exactly in a rush to go back to school and I felt mean and everything but I just wanted to be alone. Besides, Chloe had Eva and Millie to sit with so I didn't feel *that* bad about it. By the time Chloe texted me, I was already halfway to school.

I kind of knew my way around the building now, and I didn't get in trouble for forgetting books or not

doing my homework. Best of all, I didn't see Joanne Pyke all morning.

Maybe things were looking up. I skipped down the stairs to my locker and felt almost good about life, considering.

When I got there, my heart sank. A picture was stuck on the front of my locker. It was a drawing of spiders and webs with a heart and an arrow in the middle, saying

AMBER 4 MR. BATTY

A group of older girls walked past, looked at it, and laughed.

I stood in front of it feeling like my skin was on fire. Mr. Batty was this science teacher. He was about 169 years old and wore tight trousers and snakeskin shoes to school. When I looked more closely I saw a picture of a trash bin drawn in the corner.

Joanne Pyke! How did she know which locker was mine?

And then, with unbelievable timing, Locker Boy arrived. He had a heavy bag that he dropped on to

the floor, his floppy hair hanging over one eye as he bent down, his freckly nose wrinkling from the strain.

"Great drawing," he said. "Did you do it?"

He mustn't have seen the words! I pulled it down and crumpled it into a ball.

"No. S'not mine."

"Oh." He looked down at the picture, then back at me. "You okay? You've gone a bit white."

"I'm fine. It's trying hard to be the worst Monday of my life but I'm sure there'll be others that'll beat it eventually."

He laughed.

He laughed!!!

"Well, I hope I don't drop books on your head and make it worse," he said, unzipping his bag. "My locker's right above yours. What's your name? I'm Luis."

"Amber."

He nodded. "Well, I hope your day gets better, Amber," he said. And he bent down to pull books from his bag as I awkwardly sidestepped away.

I would rather have been in a shark-infested ocean than at school at that moment, but my day had got a tiny bit better already.

I left the picture scrunched in a ball on a nearby windowsill for the custodian to throw away because I couldn't face looking at a bin. Every time I went past one, I kept thinking about being shoved in there by Joanne Pyke. I even rated how dirty it was on a scale of one to ten.

When I got home after cleaning out the cats, I went into my room. I walked in and was kind of shocked to see how messy it was. I'd been so busy doing homework and writing letters and spending hours panicking, that I'd let my art area get all messed up. Usually it was shipshape. My Caran D'Ache pencils—which I keep in their box in the right color order—were just lying randomly on my desk. There were papers and old drawings everywhere and my zillions of schoolbooks were in a pile beside that. In middle school they give you hundreds of them. It's destroying the earth for sure. School should be against the law.

I needed to tidy up. I couldn't deal with the mess—not in my drawing space. And I was kind of stressed because the next day was Tuesday again, and I had Inward Reach. Joanne was going to be there and we were supposed to have a picture to give Miss Figgis. Which I had no intention of doing.

I *so* didn't want to go to school the next day. Tuesday had just become the worst day of the week. But I figured Joanne couldn't actually touch me when I was in Miss Figgis's class. I just had to avoid her everywhere else.

Which was easy.

Not.

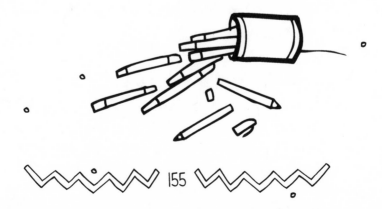

Twenty-Two–
Ventidue-Ni Jū Ni

The next morning, I had to force myself to get up. I got dressed like I was ninety-seven years old and had to keep stopping for a rest. It took ages to sort my bag out because my brain kept crashing and I had to restart it. When Chloe texted me, she was already on the bus with Eva and Millie and asked me where I was. It was her fifteenth text of the morning.

I didn't answer.

I walked to the bus stop and waited. Like a cave-woman. The bus took ages.

After first period, I met Chloe by the lockers.

"Oh, you're here," she said. "Where were you?"

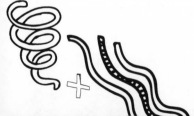

"I came in late. I...overslept."

"Oh. Did you see what Eva posted on Instagram? Hilarious!"

"I have a prehistoric phone, remember?"

"Oh yeah. Seriously, are you going to get a new one or what?"

I stuck my chin up and said, "Yes, actually. I am."

And I turned around and walked away.

I was getting a new phone. Definitely. It was only a matter of time. Knowing that made me so happy. I even tried to concentrate in French. Not that my teacher noticed.

In period four, I walked into Miss Figgis's class. I tried to be brave and cool about it but I was freaking out inside. Joanne was sitting by the window, staring out. She didn't seem to notice me so I slid into a chair and prayed it would stay that way.

"Come and sit in the circle, please, everyone," Miss Figgis said.

I gulped. Joanne was sure to notice me now. Sure enough, she got up and pulled her chair opposite mine and in the corner of my eye, I saw her give me a look that could have turned me to stone. If I hadn't been looking at the floor at the time.

Miss Figgis asked everyone to take their pictures out.

I gulped again.

The other kids were reaching into their bags. I continued inspecting the floor.

"Amber?" Miss Figgis asked. "Is there a problem?"

I raised my eyes slowly and looked at Miss Figgis. "I don't have it...one. I don't have one. Sorry."

"Everyone has to bring in a picture, Amber. This is important. No excuses. Joanne? Where's yours?"

"I stuck it up already. On a locker somewhere. Dunno where it is now," she said. I felt her eyes drilling into me. *Stone. Sto-one. Stoo-oone.* I didn't dare to look at her.

Miss Figgis wasn't very happy. "The art competition at Spit Hill is special! It is a celebration of the creative expression of the students at this school," she said, and she went on for five minutes about how it was so vital to nurture creativity in schools and blah blah and I stopped listening to her after about thirty seconds.

After her little lecture, we had to hold hands and

sing this song called "We Are Family," and then she went around the circle and asked us to name something that mattered to us.

It was torture.

Hannah said, "Umm...*X Factor*?"

This girl called Micky said, "Winning the lottery."

I didn't want to sound like I was only interested in money or anything but still I said, "Getting a new phone."

Miss Figgis flapped her hands and said, "Can you think about something more personal? An emotion, maybe? Or a person? Something that is in your heart. Joanne, your turn. What's important to you, but really, right here, in your heart?"

Joanne looked at me and said, "Revenge."

I felt that small thing inside me die again. It had died so many times it was super extra dead by now. But it still died a bit more.

"Well, we'll have to work on that, Joanne," Miss Figgis said. "And I certainly hope that comment wasn't aimed at Amber. Now, Amber and Joanne, I want your pictures tomorrow or the two of you will have an after-school detention with me. Which I would actually welcome as a chance to talk to you both."

Everything inside me went "eek."

"So pictures, please," she said, clapping her hands. "Bring them straight to the art department at eight forty-five. I'll meet you both there. On Friday they're announcing the winner! This is what you call the very last minute! No excuses. Now let's move on…"

I gulped so much in that class, I was sure my stomach was full of air and I'd die of air contamination. Maybe gulping too much is dangerous. I decided to check when I was allowed to use the computer again. Just in case.

As we walked out, Joanne mouthed, "Later, Miyamoto," and jabbed a finger at me.

I was so happy to get out of there.

When I got back home, Mum came out of her room and stood in the hallway with her arms folded.

"Hi, Mum," I said. I looked at her suspiciously. Something was up. I could just feel it.

"We need a little chat, you and me," Mum said.
Eek.

"You're not telling me anything about school and I'm getting worried."

I didn't say anything.

"Come and sit at the table. I want to hear all about it."

Bella was watching *Tangled* and even though I've seen it a gazillion times, I would much rather have sat with her. But Mum wasn't giving me that option.

So I sat and told Mum about French and math and Chloe and the other girls and all kinds of random school stuff, and then she said, "What about art?"

"Yeah, it's fine."

"What about this art competition? The deadline is tomorrow."

"How do you know about that?"

"There's a school newsletter. They send parents an email every week. Why didn't you tell me about the competition?"

Stupid newsletters. "I'm not entering," I muttered.

"Why not? You're so talented and you don't even know it. I wish I had half your talent."

I made a face. Mums always think that. You could come home with a splodge on a piece of paper that took

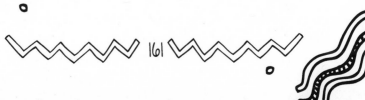

you one second to slap on with a toilet brush and your mum would think it was amazing. You can't believe anything they say when it comes to recognizing talent. Or good looks for that matter. Gregory Popov has a face like a puffer fish and his mother still calls him "gorgeous."

If there's one thing I've learned it's this: if your mum thinks you're beautiful or talented, you have to get a second opinion. Everyone's mum thinks they're the most wonderful and gorgeous genius that ever lived. Mums are great like that but you can't imagine it's the truth or anything.

"I can't do it. I just can't."

"Enter the competition," Mum said. "You could do with one of those prizes. You desperately need some new art materials and they're so expensive. Anyway, it would be good for you."

I groaned.

"Do it," she said. And she got up and walked into the kitchen.

GREGORY POPOV

162

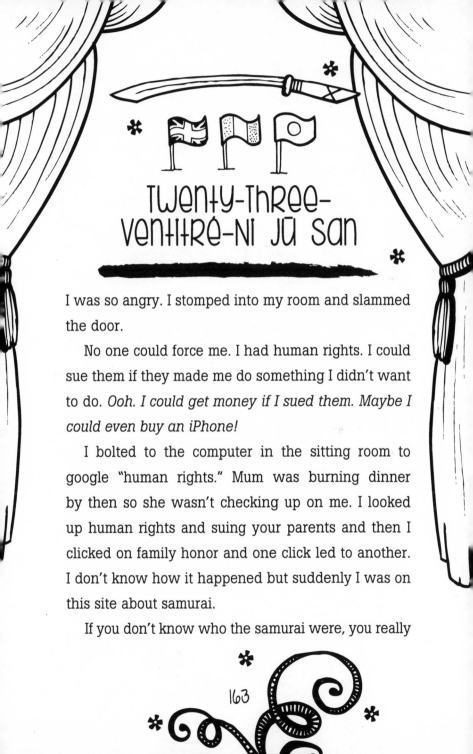

TWENTY-THREE-
VENTITRÉ-NI JŪ SAN

I was so angry. I stomped into my room and slammed the door.

No one could force me. I had human rights. I could sue them if they made me do something I didn't want to do. *Ooh. I could get money if I sued them. Maybe I could even buy an iPhone!*

I bolted to the computer in the sitting room to google "human rights." Mum was burning dinner by then so she wasn't checking up on me. I looked up human rights and suing your parents and then I clicked on family honor and one click led to another. I don't know how it happened but suddenly I was on this site about samurai.

If you don't know who the samurai were, you really

should. They were legendary warriors who protected the emperors and their clans in ancient Japan. You could only become a samurai if you were born into a samurai family, and they were super skilled at archery and fighting on horses as well as martial arts. They were *molto* cool except their hairstyles were a bit nuts. They didn't live all that long ago either. From about eight hundred years ago, they got more and more important in Japanese society until they were super respected. Then in the 1870s the ruling emperor set up a more modern army of soldiers, made up of any old blokes and not just samurai, so they kind of disappeared.

The coolest things about them though, are the legends. Samurai were known to have a really sharp sixth sense. They could sense danger and noticed everything, even tiny changes in the breeze caused by, like, a butterfly miles away stretching its wings on a leaf. They could be in a room and sense someone approaching from far. So they'd sit silently, deathly still, and wait. And then, without even looking, at exactly the moment their enemy was raising his sword to kill them, they'd whip around and slice the enemy's head off in one move.

✻ SAMURAI

And when they were captured, or if they failed in their duties, rather than be dishonored or killed by their enemies they committed *seppuku*, which is sometimes called *hara-kiri*. That little tradition was seriously disgusting. They sat on the floor, took hold of this special knife, dug it deep into their bellies and sliced it from one side to another. Then they lifted their heads so the person with them could decapitate them. There's lots of decapitation in ancient Japan. There must have been heads rolling around every-where like soccer balls.

Anyway. One part of the site was called "Samurai Clans" so I clicked on it.

I scanned through the list of the samurai clans. And then I saw something that made my eyes pop out of my head.

The name Miyamoto was on the list!

I couldn't believe it!

Miyamoto was a samurai name!

If Miyamoto was a samurai name, I was obviously a descendant of the samurai!

I couldn't stop thinking about it all through dinner. At least it took my mind off the taste of the food. I

165

couldn't wait to start doing some really cool samurai drawings, but then Mum ruined it by saying, "Do that illustration, Amber. Tonight. When you get back from Nonna's."

"But—"

"Do it."

At Nonna's I thought about samurai pretty much the entire time. Cleaning out the cats wasn't getting any easier but those latex gloves made me feel invincible. I liked them so much I wanted to start using them all the time. In the winter it would be easy because I could put them under woolly gloves and no one would know I had them on, but in the summer it would look a bit weird paying for things in shops with them on, and doing work in class.

I wasn't an expert or anything but I didn't think the cats needed cleaning out every day, sometimes twice a day. I wanted to ask Nonna about it but I was scared she'd agree with me and I'd lose my first and only job, so I kept my mouth shut.

After doing my disgusting, bacterial, toxic job, I went back home, disinfected my hands with antibacterial

gel, and put the money I had earned into the drawer. I was kind of hoping it would breed alone in there like bacteria and there'd be loads more of it every time I looked but it just wasn't happening. If I was a hot-shot scientist, I'd so develop that.

My money was adding up though. When Mum wasn't looking, I did a search on the Internet and read all about the features on my phone-to-be. There was even a small tutorial on the company website. It was so exciting.

I could almost feel that phone in my hand.

Later that evening, I went to my room and closed the door. I didn't know what to do about the art competition so I lay on my bed with my face in the pillow. Which I'd been doing a lot lately.

Then I heard something.

I looked up. You were standing above me, looking gigantic and butt-kicking, holding a raised sword. You were wearing this full body armor and a helmet with a visor, like the ancient samurai I saw on Google Images. The bottom part looked like a skirt but I didn't like to mention it.

"Amber Miyamoto," you roared, "why do you lie there defeated? We are *wushidao*: martial arts warriors of the samurai way. On behalf of the shogun himself, I command you to rise."

"Come back tomorrow," I grunted into my pillow. "I'm having a bad day."

"Tomorrow may never come. Tonight we battle against warlords who want to take our town and land. The shogun himself has summoned us. This is the ultimate honor. Rise, Miyamoto! Take your *katana*."

Katana? I had to take a look. You were holding a gleaming samurai sword. It was super shiny and had a black handle with little triangles cut out of it. It was so beautiful. Suddenly I got kind of interested.

"Rise, Miyamoto! We must battle against our enemies until death."

"Our death or their death?"

"Whichever comes first."

Eek. Death. But I'd always wanted a *katana*.

I got out my pencils and some paper and started drawing myself in the armor, known as a *do*. The leather was thick and shone with lacquer. The lead plates were heavy as rocks and the helmet fell low over my eyes. I slid my *katana* into its sheath on my belt.

I really liked being dressed like that! Samurai Amber! I drew myself with my sword raised, and then in battle with you watching my back, and us defeating armies of enemies. There were bodies on the ground left and right, and squirty blood and dying horses and thunderous clouds—I did a whole pile of pictures and I was a butt-kicking warrior in all of them.

"Yes! This is who you are, Miyamoto," you roared. "A mighty and fearless warrior of the samurai caste. Now stop sulking and give that woman a picture."

"But I don't want to give her my artwork," I whined. "I won't win and then I'll feel stupid. It's better no one ever sees it."

"Hah!" you snorted. "Failure exists only so we can see what we need to do better. Get up, samurai, and draw like you've never drawn."

You were right.

Samurai wouldn't whine and hide. They'd get on with it.

I got off the bed. "Bring it on!" I roared, grabbing more paper from my desk.

169

I drew in my room until late. I did pencil sketches and ink drawings; I experimented with color using my Caran D'Ache pencils and a brush. I was on fire. My back hurt from hunching over the desk and I got eyestrain from concentrating so hard. Hours go by in a blink when you're drawing. You can't believe it when you look at the clock and it's so late.

Just when I got too tired to carry on, you turned up again. You were sharpening your *katana*.

"Look at all these illustrations I've done!" I said. "Of me and you! I'm going to cut out this one and this one and make a collage of us defeating all these warlords."

"And you're going to enter it for the competition," you said.

"Uh-uh. I've changed my mind," I said, looking down at my drawings. "I'm not taking anything in."

"If you don't enter this competition," you said, "I'll use this sword on you."

I grinned. But knowing my work was going to be judged made me feel sick.

"Everyone will see it," I said. "It's personal. I don't want anyone to judge it and tell me what they think. And what if someone sticks the entries up on the wall? The whole school will ridicule me. They'll take photos of my picture and post it on Instagram and Facebook. All of London will laugh at me. It'll go viral on the Internet. Then they'll call in much weirder psychologists than Miss Figgis and they'll make me lie on a couch and talk about everything while they take notes and shake their heads. After that, they'll put me in a special hospital for the rest of my life."

You were squinting. I could see you weren't convinced.

"Anyway," I said, "I heard there are these twins called Max and Alex in 11B who are really talented. Everyone says one of them is going to win."

"Maybe they'll be too chicken to enter. Maybe they moved to Scotland last night. Maybe their arms fell off—"

"Okay, I get it. But still."

"Do you really want an after-school detention with Joanne Pyke and Miss Figgis? Do you? Plus, you owe Miss Figgis big-time, seeing as she saved you from the bin. Give her a picture. So what? Big deal."

I didn't like it. But you had a point.

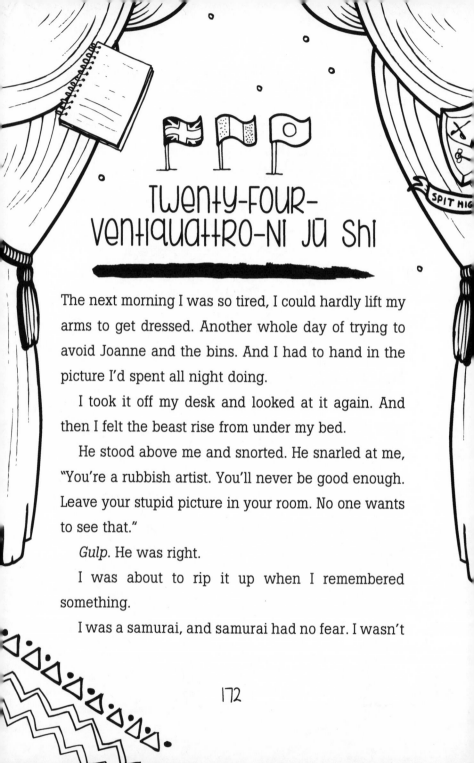

Twenty-four-
Ventiquattro-Ni Jū Shi

The next morning I was so tired, I could hardly lift my arms to get dressed. Another whole day of trying to avoid Joanne and the bins. And I had to hand in the picture I'd spent all night doing.

I took it off my desk and looked at it again. And then I felt the beast rise from under my bed.

He stood above me and snorted. He snarled at me, "You're a rubbish artist. You'll never be good enough. Leave your stupid picture in your room. No one wants to see that."

Gulp. He was right.

I was about to rip it up when I remembered something.

I was a samurai, and samurai had no fear. I wasn't

going to hide. And I wasn't going to sit through an after-school detention with Joanne and Miss Figgis because I had my honor to uphold. If I failed in this mission, I'd have to do *seppuku* in school and no one would like that very much. Someone would have to whip off my head and I can't imagine there being too many volunteers. And they'd have to clear up all the mess of intestines and blood and bits of dinner and whatever else comes out when you're in that state.

Gross.

Still, it felt like I was handing Miss Figgis a piece of my heart. I was so nervous about showing my illustration to anyone. And now I felt like I was being forced to do it. I don't get why you have to do all this stuff you don't want to and can't just have a life where you do exactly what you want and that's it.

But then maybe that's what my dad did. Just what he wanted to do. And look where that had got us all.

"Do me a favor," I said to you. "Come into school with me today. I need you."

"School won't be that bad," you said. "Sometimes the thought of something is worse than it actually is."

"And sometimes it turns out to be worse than you thought."

"True."

I ate cereal for breakfast wondering if I could ever eat a Japanese breakfast—salty fish and rice. It seemed so wrong for mornings.

Mum stood at the door folding her arms.

"Got the illustration in there, have we?" She nodded at my bag.

I said, "Nope."

"Amber—" she said, sternly.

"It's in there," I said, pointing to my portfolio, which was leaning against the wall.

She grinned. "Just don't accidentally on purpose forget that portfolio when you walk out of the door, or I'll have to follow you. You wouldn't want me running down the road after you, yelling your name like a lunatic, now would you?"

I shook my head hard.

"Thought not."

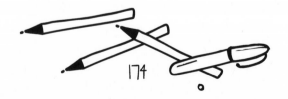

Chloe kept sending me a zillion texts to meet her at the bus stop but I didn't feel like going with her. I didn't feel like talking to anyone. Not when I was carrying my portfolio. Too many questions.

When I got near school, all my insides started freaking out. My stomach churned. I couldn't breathe properly. But walking in, I reminded myself that running in my veins was the blood of samurai.

I went straight to the art department. While I was there, I looked at the poster again.

SPIT HILL ART COMPETITION
What Matters to Me

The theme of this year's art competition is "What matters to me." We want you to encapsulate what's important for you in an illustration. We are delighted to announce that this year's judge is J. K. Gaston, a parent and well-known author and illustrator of children's books. Mrs. Gaston's books include *Popsie does a Dropsie, Moo Moo and the Martians have a Mooing Competition*, and *Dingle Dangle in a Tangle*. More famously, she is the author of *Phineas Quinn*, the best-selling book for teenagers about a boy druid, which has now been made into a blockbuster film.

Send in your entries now!

Closing date: Wednesday, 12 September

First Prize: £80 of art materials donated by the "Art Matters" organization.
Second Prize: £40 of art materials, donated by "Art Matters"
Third Prize: A trip to the Museum of Art and a set of oil paints.

Please name your entries and submit them to Mrs. Fulton in the art department.

I stared at the poster. I really wanted that prize: I could get some figurines, airbrushes, a light box, and some templates with that. But it was so scary. J. K. Gaston would be judging my picture. It was too much. I couldn't handle it.

I was about to walk away and face the detention instead when Miss Figgis arrived.

"Good morning, Amber. I was hoping you'd be here. Any sign of Joanne?"

I shook my head "I haven't seen her." I was hoping she'd got some horrible warty, pukey illness and had to move to a faraway country forever to cure herself. Or maybe she'd heard I was a samurai and had run away to hide.

"Do you have your illustration?"

What choice did I have?

I got it out of my portfolio, safely covered, and handed it to Miss Figgis with my heart and guts spilling on to the floor.

"Thank you. I'll forward it on to Mrs. Fulton in the art department."

"Can't you just keep it and not show it to her? I don't want to enter the competition or anything."

"It's fun, Amber! It doesn't have to be a Hockney! Just something from your heart."

I knew who Hockney was because Mum had taken me to his exhibition. I loved his massive paintings with blue cactuses and colorful landscapes but they were the work of a genius. Nothing like what I'd done.

My stomach sank. Of course: that was what they were looking for. Big, lively, colorful pictures and not mad collages of samurai battles and enemies with swords sticking out of them by the side of the road.

I did a long *foo* through my lips and walked to my homeroom.

Whatever. I'd done it. I'd handed it in. I could forget about it now. But it was weird knowing she had my picture. Weird knowing she'd look at it and then J. K. Gaston would too, and it would be commented on and judged. I couldn't work on it or add things to it anymore. It was fixed. Like cement. It felt so strange.

As I was walking away, Joanne slouched through the double doors of the art department.

I shrank inside myself like a tortoise, just with no shell for protection.

178

"Oh, there you are," Miss Figgis said. "I was starting to wonder. Do you have your illustration? The bell's about to go."

Joanne scowled and handed her the plastic bag she was carrying. She obviously didn't want anyone to see it either because her picture was rolled into a tube and covered in brown paper.

"Now, you two," Miss Figgis said, taking the bag and looking at us with a pouty face, "no animosity, do you hear me? We're friends, all of us in Inward Reach, and we need to support each other."

The bell went and saved me from having to answer. We all scurried off in different directions.

At first break I passed Joanne in the science building. She came right up behind me. For a moment, my heart lifted. Maybe she'd changed. Neither of us wanted to enter the art competition. We were in it together. She was going to say something nice. She was my friend.

She whispered in my ear, "Big, dirty, smelly bin. That's where you're going."

I felt my knees give way. Luckily I managed to

stay upright. I needed to talk to someone before went insane. I was shaking. I could feel the beast standing near me, and I wasn't even near my bed.

I went into the girls' toilets and shut the door of a cubicle.

"I'm freaking out here," I whispered. "I'm really losing it. I need you."

You turned up. You were dressed head to foot in hard-core protective clothing, like you were working in a nuclear reactor. It was a bit over the top. The toilets were bad but they weren't *that* bad.

"Not my favorite location to meet in, I have to say."

"Sorry, but this is an emergency. She's trying to get me in a bin. What do I do? I'm scared. Even the beast under my bed isn't as scary as her."

The beast entered the shadowy place in my mind and snorted with anger. But it was true.

"Shame we don't have a zap gun," you said. "We could blast her and turn her to dust."

I looked at you. "I'm serious."

"So am I!"

"Don't you have a plan B?"

"No, because zapping her is a brilliant plan A. You

want some advice? Don't be scared. Be strong and stand up for yourself. You'll be fine."

You were right. Hiding in the toilets was no behavior for a samurai.

"Now let's get out of here," you said. "I hate toilets. I don't need to use them because I'm a figment of your imagination, so I sure as moose dung don't want to hang out in them."

For the rest of the day, I walked around like a hunted animal. I used to see them on David Attenborough programs, being attacked by an eagle or a lion. Usually you felt excited for the lion. When he finally catches the deer after carefully stalking it for ages and then sprinting wildly after it, you wanted to cheer, like my mum and Nonna do when Italy scores in the World Cup. *Wooh! Victory!* But you never think of the poor deer that's running terrified and gets ripped apart and eaten alive.

Now I knew how they felt. Poor hunted animals. Having to watch your back all the time. Living in fear of something attacking you. It's not a great way to live, I can tell you.

Just before I went home, I saw Luis, the Locker Boy.

"How's it going?" he asked. "Had a worse day yet?"

"Actually, yes. Every day gets a little bit worse than the one before."

His lip curled into a smile and his kind brown eyes locked with mine for a second. I think he felt my pain. I think he saw a fellow hunted animal and felt sorry for me. "I don't like it here much either," he said. He picked up a small portfolio that had been leaning against the wall and walked off.

I nearly fell over.

He had a portfolio!

He was an artist like me!

I couldn't get it out of my mind.

I thought about what was in that portfolio while I was cleaning out the cats at Nonna's house and all through karate. I managed to remember my *kata*, but when the teacher got out his squidgy baseball bat, I started thinking about the portfolio again.

Had Locker Boy entered the art competition? What if he was *molto* talented? Was my picture babyish? What if he did brilliantly happy Hockney-type artwork

182

and not mad multilayered collages with painted stuff all over the top? I started thinking about all the things I should have done instead. I should have done something happy and cheerful.

What was in that portfolio?

Would I ever find out?

WHACK!

Crash!

"Amber," my karate teacher said, standing over me as I lay on the floor. "You're not concentrating!"

Of course I wasn't. Even mind-focused samurai masters daydream sometimes.

TWENTY-FIVE-VENTICINQUE-NI JŪ GO

When I got home, Bella handed me another letter.

"I think that's enough now, Bella," I said. "You should give Dad a chance to get used to your letters, and not…you know…bombard him."

"He likes it, I told you. And anyway, this one's really important."

This was getting silly. I had to do something about it. But with the art competition and Joanne Pyke and everything else going on, Bella and her letters had been pushed to the back back backest part of my mind.

When I got into my room, I opened it.

Dier Dad.
I couden't find to socks the saym
this mornig. This is why we need
you heare.
Love, Bella

Socks. That's what she thought was really important!

But maybe Bella was right. We needed a dad not just for all the big things, like buying us stuff and taking us out and giving us advice. We needed him for all the zillions of small things too.

I wrote back to her straight away and put it in my drawer to give her in a day or two.

Dear Bella,

Ask your mum to help you find socks. I can't come back just to do that. I'm trying to save the world over here. Or just buy loads the same color so you can always find a pair.

Love,

Bella didn't even bother waiting for the reply. Later that evening, she stood in front of me. She pulled something out of her shirt and gave me another letter. I hadn't even put the last one in an envelope yet.

I sighed, went to my room and opened it. *Really. What now?*

Dier Dad.

If I joine the scool kwaya will you come and here me sing? I want you to come overwise there's no pointe. And wil yu teache me how to mak a good card tower? Mine kieps falling down. so I neid you.
Love. Bella.

Bella was so weird.

I couldn't draw that evening after the drawing frenzy the night before, so instead I stared into space and thought about Bella's letters. I had to do something to sort that problem out. And after a while it came to me. The answer seemed obvious.

I wasn't going to write back to her anymore.

186

It was just making things worse.

I knew she'd be upset about it but she left me no choice.

After I finished my homework, I got ready for bed and lay there thinking about my dad. I was annoyed with him for doing this to Bella. The black hole inside me started swirling again, darkly and silently. I tried to breathe deeply so it wouldn't suck all the air out of my lungs. I don't know how much time went by.

Mum came in to put laundry away. It was quiet in the house. Bella was in bed. I must have looked dark and silent myself because Mum said, "What's up with *you*?"

I shrugged. "Nothing."

"Right. So why have you got steam coming out of your ears?"

I pulled myself up and looked in the mirror. My forehead was in a knot and my lips were snarling. No steam though.

"It's an expression, Amber. What's the matter?"

I stood by the mirror a little longer. I was checking if I could see my dad in my face, because if I could,

I wanted a new face. Maybe I didn't get his face at all but, like, chunky fingers or a hairy back. Great. Or maybe I didn't get something you could see, but a gene of brilliance and when I got older I'd discover I was a computer genius or a world-champion racecar driver. Or maybe I got the gene of weirdness that would make me walk out on my kids too when I grew up.

Nah.

No way.

I sat on the edge of my bed, wondering if my dad even cared what a mess he'd left behind.

"Amber, what is it?" Mum said.

I stared at my reflection and muttered, "Why did he leave?"

Mum knew who I meant.

"Oh," she said. "That's what's bothering you."

She stopped putting the pile of clothes away, closed the wardrobe door and sat on the floor with her back against it. I could hear clapping from Mr. Venables's telly through the floor. Mum's head was tilted back so it was resting on the door and she folded a sock around her hand again and again, smoothing it like she was stroking a pet. Then she sighed so hard all her body lifted and then sank.

"It wasn't anything to do with you, Amber. He didn't leave *you*."

"Yeah, he did."

"Yeah, well, he did, but it wasn't because of you. You didn't do anything. I told you—he loved you. And I'm sure he still does."

I didn't want Mum to see the tears in my eyes so I turned my head the other way. I just didn't get it. It made no sense at all.

I didn't tell her what I was thinking. He couldn't have loved me that much. Maybe if I'd been a boy he'd have stayed. Maybe if I'd been a cooler kid he'd have been so proud of me he wouldn't have been able to rip himself away. Maybe if I'd been a genius at math or an amazing piano player he'd still be at home. Or he'd have taken me too.

"You don't leave someone if you love them," I said.

It was so quiet I could hear Mum breathing. It was one of those times where your thoughts sit around you like a blanket and you're weighed down by them. Even the air felt heavy, and it made me wonder whether it felt like that in a vacuum or whether vacuums were actually really light.

"Life is more complicated than you think," Mum said after a while. "Nothing is black and white."

"What does that mean?" I asked, turning to look at her.

"When you get older you'll understand. It's hard to figure out how adults think when you're a kid. It's hard enough when you're an adult. Life is so confusing and human beings are strange creatures, Amber. They're complicated. Illogical.".

I didn't say anything for a bit. But then it just came out. "He can't have been very cool. Someone cool wouldn't have done that."

She sucked on her teeth. I knew that if she got the chance she would have strangled him. She had to bring us up alone and she had no one to help her. No one to share the bills with her or fix the sink when it broke. No one to help her decide whether Bella was really too ill to go to school that day or if she was just pretending. Mum had to make every decision on her own. She worked hard every day and we still had no money. And she had to be everything to us.

She could easily have told me all the bad things about him. I knew she had a whole list of them. But she didn't.

I was glad because right then I really didn't want to hear them. I wanted to think, just for one minute, that despite all the things I'd just said, he was perfect after all. I wanted to believe that instead of him deciding to go, it was this messed-up world that forced him out of our lives, against his will. That he got pulled away screaming, his arms outstretched reaching toward us, his eyes full of despair. Something dramatic like that. Otherwise, I just couldn't get it.

"No one's perfect," she said. "When you get older you'll understand that life is about choices. Your dad made his choice and now he has to live with it."

I had to think about that for a minute.

"What choice does he have to live with?" I said.

She paused. Somewhere in the distance a siren started wailing.

"He's missing out."

"On what?"

"On the greatest gift of all. Better than anything."

I had a feeling I knew what she was going to say. But I asked anyway.

"What is it?"

"You."

I'd never thought of myself as a gift before. "Me? Just me? Or Bella as well?"

"Bella as well. Gifts, plural."

"But we get sick and you have to find someone to look after us so you can work and we grow out of our shoes all the time and we drive you crazy and there are a whole bunch of things you'd love to do but you can't because you have to look after us."

Mum smiled. "Don't kid yourself, honey. You two are the best thing that ever happened to me. I'm blessed, and you know why? Because I get to spend every single day with you, watching you grow into the most amazing people on the planet. Your dad is missing out on all that. His choice. His loss."

The air felt even heavier and the black hole kept swirling. After a while I said, "Mum?"

"Mmm?"

"Do you think someone should tell him that? Because maybe, once he realizes what he's missing, he'll come back."

Mum touched her fingers to the corners of her eyes.

DREAM 192

I think she was trying not to cry. For me. She cleared her throat and said quietly, "I doubt that very much. He knew what he was walking away from. But it's a shame. You two need him so badly."

I felt my face sting.

Mum got up and stroked my head. Then she said good night and left my room, her sad-sounding footsteps shuffling across the floor.

I didn't tell her about you.

You sat on the end of my bed when she went out. You weren't a sumo wrestler or a samurai this time. Instead you were a nice old doctor in a white coat with glasses on your nose.

I looked at the ceiling and bit my lip.

"It's all right to cry," you said. "You need to wash the stale tears out or you could get chronic globbi-itis. That's when tears get globby from sitting in your eyes too long. And if you're not careful, it could lead to tear poisoning, which is the most painful form of death there is. Better to let them flow out and then your body can produce new ones. You don't want to die like that, believe me."

I looked at you and raised my eyebrows.

"Trust me. I'm a doctor. I've seen it before. If you don't believe me you can google it. Google 'globbi-itis' and see what comes up."

I would have gone out to the computer, but I still wasn't allowed to use it, technically. So I let the tears out. You know, just so it wouldn't get all globby in there. The last thing I needed was tear poisoning when I had so many other things to worry about.

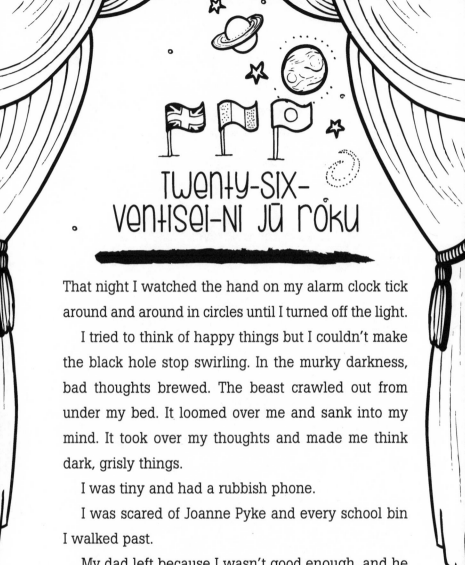

TWENTY-SIX–
VENTISEI–NI JŪ ROKU

That night I watched the hand on my alarm clock tick around and around in circles until I turned off the light.

I tried to think of happy things but I couldn't make the black hole stop swirling. In the murky darkness, bad thoughts brewed. The beast crawled out from under my bed. It loomed over me and sank into my mind. It took over my thoughts and made me think dark, grisly things.

I was tiny and had a rubbish phone.

I was scared of Joanne Pyke and every school bin I walked past.

My dad left because I wasn't good enough, and he stayed away because everything in his life was more interesting than I was. He was never going to come back, and I'd never get to hang out with him. Not ever. He didn't care about me and he never would.

My artwork was pathetic and everyone in school would crack up when they saw it and they'd ALL try and dump me in a bin, even the teachers.

I lay there for a long time with my nose just out of the covers.

Maybe I'd stay there forever. Like that French writer Mum told me about who stayed in bed for the last fourteen years before he died. I'd do my art lying down and not bother to get up at all, except to eat and go to the toilet.

With the beast in my mind, everything seemed too scary to deal with.

Just as I thought that, you stood over me. You were dressed in a stripy black-and-white top and a black hoodie, just like mine.

"Hey!" I whispered. "Those are my clothes!"

"Shh." You were holding my *katana*.

"What are you doing?" I whispered.

"You've got to kill that beast."

"Me? Are you crazy? It's big and evil. It'll kill me."

"You're going to come out here now, samurai, and slice its fat ugly head off."

I could see the beast's horns glistening in the moonlight. I heard it snorting.

"But it hates me. It takes control of my head and makes me feel bad about myself," I whispered.

"No one can make you feel bad about yourself unless you let them."

I paused for a second to digest that.

You were right!

I allowed that beast to be there and do that to me.

I needed a green, furry, friendly beast living under my bed that told me good things and made me feel good about myself instead of this ugly, evil one. It was a bit too much like a green, furry version of my mum though.

I'd had enough. I wasn't going to let it make me feel bad anymore.

I was going to kill the beast.

I shot out from under the covers, took the *katana* and stood on my bed looking scary in my Bart Simpson pajamas.

I was filled with strength—nothing was going to

make me feel small and powerless again, not unless I let it.

"Beast of Darkness Who Lives Under my Bed and in the Shadowy Places in my Mind," I bellowed in my most solemn and bloodcurdling voice. "Your days are over!"

The beast snorted furiously. He was huge. He roared in his deep dark voice, "You think you can slay a giant, angry, snarling creature like me? You can't even **draw** a beast as great as me!"

That was it. No one spoke to me like that.

I swung the sword above my head. The beast roared and charged at me. I nearly turned and ran screaming, but instead I held my breath, aimed, and thrust the sword through the air and into the beast's huge chest with a mighty whack. Then, as he howled and shrieked, I pulled it out, turned it sideways with two hands and, just before I swung it again, I hollered, "I can draw ANYTHING! I AM THE GREATEST ARTIST ALIVE!" and I sliced his head off and he fell to the ground with a thunderous crash.

The silence in my room and in my head was unbelievable.

And then I felt this enormous surge of happiness and screamed, "YES!" and jumped up and down on my bed in victory because the gruesome monster was dead! I had killed it myself, and it was never coming back.

After that, it all seemed much clearer.

I figured out how to solve the problem of Bella's letters and her party. And I decided to pluck up the courage to talk to Luis the Locker Boy, because if anyone understood how I felt in that school, I figured he did. Plus, I was desperate to know what was in his portfolio.

And I wasn't going to worry about my competition entry anymore. Who cared about that stupid competition anyway?

With the beast dead, it all fell into place.

But the jumping up and down on my bed must have been quite noisy, even though most of the shouting was done in my head.

"Amber?" Mum asked, sticking her half-asleep face through my door. "Why are you jumping up and down on your bed at eleven thirty at night?"

"It's okay, Mum, everything's good now. It'll all be fine. You'll see."

TWenty-seven-ventisette-ni Jū Shichi

Just before I left the house the next day, I caught Bella looking through the mail.

"Have you seen anything for me?" she asked as I walked past.

"Nope."

She made a face and stomped off.

Good.

I picked up my bag and went to school feeling victorious. With a bit of terror trying to sneak in from the sides. But mainly victorious. I talked to Chloe, Eva, and Millie on the bus, even though I didn't have cool things to show them on my phone. They showed me theirs and I didn't even feel like a loser cavegirl.

I told myself I was part of a fearless warrior clan and nothing could hurt me. Even if it wasn't true.

I didn't really hear anything the teachers said in the morning classes. I was thinking of killing the beast and how great it felt, slicing its head off. I was glad no one asked me what was on my mind or they'd have thought I was a nutso psychopath.

Then, when the bell rang and we went out for break, I noticed something. There was a buzz around the school. Kids were chattering excitedly in the corridors.

The results must have come out for the art competition. That was fine. I remained cool and calm. But still, I had to check.

I went to the art department. My eyes were pulled toward the crowd of kids standing around the bulletin board. I heard them saying, "Who? Who won?"

"What do you mean he came third?"

"Where's the picture that won?"

"It's INSANE! You've got to see it!"

They were jostling and elbowing each other but being small, I could squeeze in between them, right to the front, between their arms.

When I got near enough, I saw it. It was a big poster.

It said:

SPIT HILL ART COMPETITION
RESULTS!

Winner: "Warrior" by Amber Miyamoto
Runner-Up: "The Future" by Max Tropp
Third Place: "Claire" by Jamie Bright
Highly Commended: "Revenge" by Joanne Pyke

A HUGE **WELL DONE** TO ALL THE ENTRANTS FROM MRS. FULTON AND THE ART DEPARTMENT!

We would like to congratulate the winners and thank all those who entered this year's excellent competition. The standard was very high and it was extremely hard to judge!

I stood there staring at the wall.

Me?

I won?

"Amber Miyamoto?" a girl behind me said. "Who *is* that? It sounds like a Japanese name or something."

"Bright came THIRD?" someone front of me said. "What about Max Tropp? I was sure he was going to win."

Then someone yelled excitedly, "Whoa! Look at that picture! It's *SICK*! Is that, like, a Japanese super-hero or something? That's wicked!"

And then I saw it. Our artwork was displayed on the next bulletin board. Mine was in the middle with the word "WINNER" across the top.

I was unable to move or speak, feeling probably the most overcome I'd ever felt in my entire life.

Max Tropp's was an awesome charcoal drawing of a super-tech robot. It was so good! Jamie Bright's was a portrait of a girl looking down at a table. Even Joanne Pyke's was on the wall. It was another of her scary pictures in the same style as the picture on my locker. It was dark and swirly and violent and had scary faces in it and in the middle, someone with a screamy tortured face, like that famous Edvard Munch painting. But it was good.

"Do you reckon that Amber girl really did it?" a boy beside me said to his friend. "She's only in sixth grade."

"Yeah, she probably, like, paid some artist to do it and she's pretending it's hers."

Their voices washed over me. I just stood there in a daze.

Just then, the bell rang. Everyone in the corridor started leaving for classes.

I stood and stared at my picture until I was the only one left. I was still acting like a brainless zombie when Miss Figgis rushed down the corridor.

"Amber! Hah haaa! There you are!"

She ran over to me and gave me a huge hug, which I didn't think teachers were allowed to do and is probably against the law or something. Then she said, "Congratulations, Amber! Your drawing is *magnificent*! And I have amazing news for you! Mrs. Gaston wants to speak to you! Do you know who she is?"

"Yeah...ummm...isn't she the woman who judged the competition?"

"Absolutely, and she's also J. K. Gaston, famous writer and illustrator of children's books. She wrote *Phineas Quinn and the Pyramids of Pain*, which, as you probably know, sold millions!"

"Oh...yeah. *Phineas Quinn* is pretty amazing."

"Amber, she thinks YOU are amazing. She wants to talk to you about doing an illustration for her new book, which will be published next year!"

"Me?"

"You! And besides that, we all agreed that your drawing is without a doubt the most outstanding entry we've ever had in our competition. You're an extremely talented artist, Amber. I think you have a wonderful future ahead of you."

My throat got all bunged up like someone had stuffed socks down there. My eyes stung with disbelief.

"Thank you, Miss Figgis," I said, once I swallowed the socks. I turned around to leave but there was something on my mind. "Can I just ask you something?"

"Of course you can."

"What's with the additional prize?"

"It's for Joanne's very special entry, 'Revenge,' a postmodern punk medley full of emotion and angst, which we thought was fabulous. We decided it deserved special consideration."

I shuddered. I was hoping the person in the picture wasn't supposed to be me and wishing I could actually talk to Joanne about art and not only about trash bins. At least we had something in common.

And then the bell rang.

Twenty-Eight-
Ventotto-Ni Jū Hachi

I don't remember anything that happened in the next class. I was in a dream.

The judges didn't throw my illustration in the bin.

I'd won the art competition.

J. K. Gaston wanted to talk to me about doing an illustration for her new book.

People thought my picture was sick and insane, which at my school is a good thing.

I felt freaked out that my illustration was exposed on a big board, and Joanne Pyke's theme scared the life out of me. But at the same time, it was the closest to heaven I'd ever been.

By lunchtime, everyone seemed to have worked out

who I was. Kids were crowding around me in the corridor asking me if I really did it. One girl said, "Will you do the invitations for my birthday party?"

"You've got to be joking!" someone answered. "She's a pro! You're gonna pay top dollar for that!"

"How come you're not famous?"

"How did a little kid like you learn to *draw* like that?"

Then, on the way to French, a huge boy walked up to me. He looked like a double-decker bus with a uniform on. For one terrible moment, I thought he might be another Pyke.

He stuck out his hand. I shook it because he wasn't the kind of boy you said no to.

"Nice one," he said with a grin. "I'm Max Tropp. Your picture is *sick*."

"You think so?" I said, *molto* relieved. "Wow! Thanks. Yours is awesome as well."

"How come you don't come to art club?" he asked. It was kind of hard to look at him because it made my neck hurt—he was about ten feet taller than me.

"Art club?"

"Yeah, Wednesdays after school. But we hang out most lunchtimes as well."

"I didn't know there was art club."

"I did put a poster up about it but I found it scrunched up on the windowsill. It had 'Amber 4 Mr. Batty' drawn on the back. Actually, thinking about it, it looked like one of Joanne's drawings. So, I straightened it out and put it back up but maybe you didn't see it."

I smiled. "I think I only saw the other side of it."

"So come today," he said. "At lunchtime. You'll be our guest of honor."

I wondered if Locker Boy would be there but I didn't want to ask.

"Okay then."

"Well, okay then," he said with a grin. And he walked off.

After he left I wondered whether Joanne Pyke went to art club because if she did, I might have to avoid it.

But at lunchtime, I couldn't help it: I had to go to the art department to check it out.

Through the glass in the door I could see Max and a bunch of others sitting around the big table, eating sandwiches, and talking. I pushed the door open.

The table was covered with paper, pencils, inking pens, brushes, paint pots, colored pencils: it was the most beautiful sight ever. My eyes went *ahh* and my heart went *ahh* and every cell in me went *ahh* as well. If you don't like art, you won't get that, but if you do, you'll know just what I mean. If there'd been a camera on my stupid phone *that* was what I would have taken a photo of to post on Instagram. It was an artist's dream come true.

As I walked in, they all turned around and smiled at me. I went bright red. Max came over, patted me on the back, and then introduced me to everyone: Jamie Bright, who came third; Max's twin brother, Alex, also huge, obviously; and about ten other people whose names I wasn't sure I'd ever remember.

Luis the Locker Boy wasn't there, but I was too shy to ask about him.

"Um...does Joanne Pyke come to art club?" I asked nervously.

"Yeah, sometimes," Jamie said, "when she's not sticking people in bins."

Eek. They knew about that?

Jamie grinned. "You don't have worry about her anymore. Max and Alex told her to leave you alone and she won't mess with them. Anyway, she thought your picture was wicked."

"She did?"

"Everyone did."

My heart flipped up and out of me. I sat down at the table and we talked about my illustration style, and theirs, and which pencils we preferred and why we liked the paper we used and what kind of things we liked drawing.

It was soooo cool! When do I ever get a chance to talk about stuff like that? About shadowing and perspective and shading and paper? I was so happy. I had friends. I had *homies*. Okay, they weren't half Japanese and half Italian, but they were from the same weird tribe as me. I could just feel it.

It felt like I'd come home.

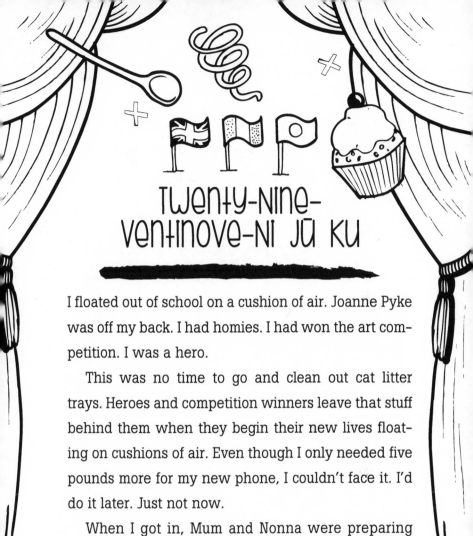

Twenty-Nine-Ventinove-Ni Jū Ku

I floated out of school on a cushion of air. Joanne Pyke was off my back. I had homies. I had won the art competition. I was a hero.

This was no time to go and clean out cat litter trays. Heroes and competition winners leave that stuff behind them when they begin their new lives floating on cushions of air. Even though I only needed five pounds more for my new phone, I couldn't face it. I'd do it later. Just not now.

When I got in, Mum and Nonna were preparing for Bella's party. Nonna said, "*Ciao, Ambra, amore. Come stai?*" and I said, "Fine, thanks," instead of "*Bene, grazie,*" so Nonna started shouting at my Mum because we don't speak Italian at home.

"Mannaggia! Perché queste bambine non parlano Italiano?"

Mum was yelling, "Oh, for goodness sake! They live *here* and they're half Japanese! They understand—they just won't speak it!" but Nonna wasn't happy. She moaned about it as she baked cupcakes and lasagna and generally made the whole house smell amazing. Mum rolled her eyes and whispered, "Do me a favor, Amber. Next time, just say *'Bene, grazie,'* okay?"

Then Mum carried on wrapping big parcels in newspaper and asking Nonna why her Jell-O didn't set when she did exactly what it said on the packet.

Bella was icing the cupcakes. I took one look at how she was doing them—all thick and sloppy with pink icing—and wondered whether letting Bella do it was a good idea. Icing cupcakes is a fun job except the icing was too pink for my liking. Why anyone likes pink is beyond me. It's the color of puke mixed with blood and pus. I told Bella that and she shouted, "MUM!! Amber's being disgusting!"

Hehehehe.

I didn't want to tell them about the competition but at the same time, I really, really did.

I didn't say anything straight away though. I waited until we sat down to eat. As usual, Mum asked me how my day was. So I said, "Yeah, umm...soooo... well, you know there was, like, that art competition? At school? And that's why Miss Figgis wanted us to give her pictures?"

"You did give her one, didn't you?" Mum asked, raising one eyebrow.

I nodded.

"Good," Mum said. "Go on."

I looked at the table and fiddled with my fork. "Well, loads of people entered and some of the entries were so good—"

"It doesn't matter that you didn't win, Amber; it's only your first year. I'm just glad you gave a picture in. That's a big step for you. There'll be lots more competitions."

I sat there with a cheesy smile on my face.

"What? Why are you looking at me like that?" Mum asked.

"'Cause...umm..."

"Amber, spit it out, will you?"

"I...won the art competition."

"You *what?*" Mum yelled. "Aaarrrrgghhhhh!"

She got up from her chair, grabbed me off mine, lifted me up in the air, and spun me around. She was screeching and hollering and yelling, "That's AMAZING!!!! You see? I *told* you! Ahahahaaaa!"

Once Mum put me down, Nonna grabbed me and yelled things in Italian and smothered me until I could hardly breathe, then started dancing around the kitchen holding my hands, which would have been *molto* embarrassing if anyone I knew had seen me. We hadn't even finished our pasta yet. All that time Bella was clapping and cheering but then she felt a bit left out, so she started pulling my mum's jumper and saying, "I'm really good at art as well, aren't I, Mum? AREN'T I, MUM? MUM!"

Once Mum and Nonna calmed down and wiped their eyes, I remembered the stupid cats. So I said, "Oh, Nonna. Your cats! I really don't feel like doing your cats today. Can I have a day off and clean them out tomorrow?"

"*Amore,*" Nonna said. "No cats today! You don't need to come no more. *Lo faccio io.* I do it. Iss no problem."

It was a great offer but I really needed that last five pounds.

214

"One last time, Nonna."

"I think you start like *i miei gatti*, huh? Huh?" she said, grinning.

Do not be under any illusions, I wanted to say. *If I had my way, I would slice your stupid cats' heads off and boil them in a bucket full of acid.*

But I didn't tell her that.

She got her bag, pulled out her purse and handed me the last five pounds I needed.

"Wait—why are you giving me this? What about your litter trays?"

"*Non fa niente*, Ambra. Iss no problem," Nonna said, waving her hand. "I do cats myself. I no have problem clean them. Juss you mamma, she tell me you need job, so I give you job."

No! All those days of cleaning cat poo and she was just doing me a favor. I could have watered plants! I could have—

"Anyway," Nonna continued, "today I buy something good. *Molto conveniente.* Is call "litter liner." Is plastic bag—have nice smell—for put in litter tray. Now I just lift the bag and it take out all the dirty litter. Then put new bag. *È facile!* Iss easy."

215

I didn't know whether to laugh or cry. All that disgusting scraping. And all along there were things called litter liners.

I bit my lip. But at least now I had the money.

All of it.

It felt so good.

After dinner, even though I'd counted it about a hundred times, I did it again, just to make sure. I checked the price of what I was buying online and put the money away until the next morning. As soon as the shops opened, I was going down there and buying exactly what I'd been saving for.

Thirty–
Trenta–san jū

When I got up the next morning, Bella was sitting on a chair by the front door.

"What are you doing?" I asked sleepily.

"Waiting for the mailman."

"Still no letters?"

"Nope."

"Aw, that's a shame. Never mind."

Once I'd had breakfast and was showered and dressed, I put my money in my purse and went with Nonna to the shops. I spent ages and ages looking at the phones and dreaming about holding every single one of them in my hand. I looked at their functions and the minutes and data plans and which accessories you could get with them. Even Nonna got bored

waiting for me and she's one of those people who can spend all day in the same shop. So she went off to the pharmacy and I said I'd meet her there.

Eventually, I chose what I wanted, bought it with my hard-earned cash, and walked out of there feeling great. Like an adult. Like a real and valid person.

When we got home, Mum asked, "What did you buy? Got yourself a new phone by any chance?"

"*Forse*," I said with a satisfied smile. "Maybe. You'll see soon enough."

Nonna had to go home to feed her cats, so I put my shopping in my room.

When I came back out, I saw Bella sitting in her pink palace looking even moodier than before.

I ignored her and went into the sitting room to watch TV.

I could hear Bella going and checking the mail again and again and then stomping back to her pink palace in a big huff.

After not very long at all, she appeared at the doorway.

I was watching a show about eagles hunting foxes.

It was usually the kind of show I liked but I wanted to rescue the poor fox.

"Amber," she said.

"Mmm."

"Maybe Dad's letter arrived but it got put some-where by mistake."

"Nothing's arrived as far as I know. Sorry."

Her bottom lip wobbled and her eyes got really big and sad, like the cat in *Shrek*.

I almost felt sorry for her but told myself not to. It couldn't go on. My secret drawer was getting full and Bella's party was the next day. I just couldn't let her think he was coming.

She went back to her room but came back after about five minutes and handed me an envelope. I wasn't watching TV anyway. I couldn't concentrate. Not with Bella marching around like that. So I took it and told her I'd mail it for her just as soon as I got my shoes on.

When I went to my room, I opened it.

Dier Dad,
    Do yu ever mis us? And do yu
    ever mis Mum?
                Love, Bella

Even if I was still writing back to her—which I wasn't—what could I have said in reply to that? I wanted my dad to miss us. And I wanted him to miss my mum so badly and feel like he'd made the worst mistake of his life leaving her. But I didn't imagine Bella would ever think of asking that question.

Because Mum had been so busy organizing the party, dinner was soggy noodles and hard veggie burgers. When I become a loaded artist, I am so getting a chef.

"Come on then, Bella," Mum said after dinner, "bath time."

"Don't want a bath," Bella grumbled.

"But I'll put in your bubbles and your wind-up toys that swim and—"

"Don't want bubbles."

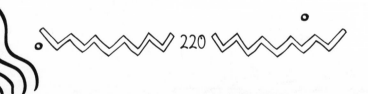

"You need to wash your hair, Bella. And you love having a bath! It'll be fun."

"Don't like fun," Bella grumbled. "Don't like baths. Don't like hair."

Mum looked at me and stretched her eyes wide. I felt sorry for Mum because she had no idea why Bella was being so difficult. I knew she was behaving like that because she wasn't getting any replies but I wasn't going to tell Mum that.

Mum fought with Bella in the bath for an hour trying to wash her hair and ended up getting annoyed with her.

I stayed well out of the way.

When it was Bella's bedtime, I saw her lying on the floor near the window in her palace of pink. She looked empty, like a teddy with no stuffing.

I had to talk to her about it, so I stuck my head in. "What are you doing down there?"

She didn't answer me.

"Bella? You can tell me. What's wrong?" I walked into her room and sat down next to her on the floor.

She was quiet for a while. Then she looked at me and said, "He didn't write back."

221

"Oh. Well, maybe you asked him something he couldn't answer."

"No."

"Maybe you didn't listen to what he was trying to tell you."

Bella squinted suspiciously. I had to be careful.

She was quiet for a while and then said, "He doesn't love me anymore."

Oh no. I'd really done it this time.

"Bella, it's not that. Maybe he just didn't get your letters yet. Or maybe he's been too busy to reply."

She rolled away from me and stared at the bedpost. I couldn't see her face.

"Bella, the fact you got letters from him is amazing. It should make you happy, but don't expect them. Maybe they were, like, a special one-time-only gift. Maybe he'll never write to you again."

"But I thought he was going to come home," she whimpered without turning around.

It was then that I realized what a huge mistake I'd made and how bad my genius idea had been. Instead of making her feel better, I'd made everything worse. I'd got her hopes up and now I'd let her down again.

I needed to tell her the truth. I had to tell her that it was me all along.

But I just couldn't do it. Poor Bella. She had so much confusion still ahead of her. She might have been annoying and crazy and weird, but she was my sister. I had to at least try and help her out.

"Bella?"

"Mmm?"

"Can you turn around? I want to tell you something."

She turned around and lay there, looking at me with her huge brown eyes.

It was really hard to tell her nice things. It almost killed me. But I did it anyway.

"You know how much we love you? Mum and me?"

She showed a space of about an inch between her thumb and her forefinger. "About this much?"

I smiled. "Way more. We love you more than the sky and the earth and the animals and the birds. More than chocolate ice cream, more than birthdays, and more than most of the universe."

"More than movies with popcorn?"

"More than movies with popcorn."

"More than art?"

I had to think about that for a second.

"Yes. But only just."

She grinned and sat up.

"And I want you to know that you might not have a daddy anymore, but you do have a big sister. And I promise you I will look after you forever and ever, even when we're big and married and have our own kids."

Her bottom lip began to quiver and her eyes filled with tears. "It's not the same, Amber."

"I know."

"You can't teach me to catch spies."

I smiled. "Course I can."

"Really? Will you come and hear me sing in the choir?"

"If you want."

"Can I sit on your knee in the sandpit?"

I had to draw the line there. "No, because it's dirty."

"So I still need my daddy."

"I know you need your daddy, Bella, but he's gone. But we have Mum and Nonna and each other. So don't be sad about not getting a letter. Okay?"

Big tears fell down her cheeks. I put my arm around her (at least she'd had a bath and wasn't sticky and full of germs) and stared out of the window at the moon. I remembered what she'd said about the moon being a mirror and him looking up at it, wherever he was, and it made me wonder where he was and what he was doing right at that moment. I mean, he was still alive and out there somewhere, programming computers, drinking tea, tying his shoelaces every morning. Looking up at the same moon we were looking up at.

"Amber?"

"What?"

"Do you think he'll ever come home?"

I wanted to tell her that I hoped not because I didn't think I could ever forgive him. I felt like I would never trust him and there was a black hole sucking the air out of me when I thought about him. But there was a part of me that wanted to believe he would. Not for me. But because Bella needed him.

So I said, "I dunno, Bella. I wouldn't count on it. But don't think about that now. It's your party tomorrow. You need to be happy."

We sat for a bit without saying anything. Then I kissed her on the top of her head (even though it was wet and shampoo-y) and went to my room.

Thirty-one-
Trentuno-San Jū Ichi

When I lay on my bed that night, I was half sad about Bella and half so happy, my heart was pushing up out of my chest. It felt like it would go right through the ceiling and fly up up up into the stars and sail around the universe if I didn't put my hand there to stop it.

You lay down beside me, dressed as a normal kind of dad, for once. In a blue hoodie and jeans. With one Wednesday sock on and one Monday sock, even though it wasn't Wednesday *or* Monday.

You looked at me, grinning.

"I won the art competition," I whispered. "I can't believe it."

"Course you did. Didn't doubt it for a second. How're you feeling?"

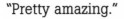

"Pretty amazing."

"Good. You deserve it. And you killed the beast under your bed."

"I know, right? And I have you in my life. My dream dad."

"Yup. Life is all rosy and perfect, eh?"

I sighed. "Not exactly. I tricked Bella and upset her. I don't feel good about *that.* And writing those letters made me think about my real dad, and that's made me angry."

"Why angry?"

"Because he walked out and he doesn't even care if we're alive or dead."

"Amber," you said, "you need to forgive him for that."

My teeth ground together. *Me? Forgive him?* "No way. Why should I?"

"'Cause if you carry all that anger around in your heart it'll come out sometime. Maybe at the world, maybe at someone you love. Maybe even at everyone you meet. Trust me, you don't want that anger sitting in there drilling a hole in your heart."

I thought about that. But it was way more complicated than that.

I stared at the floor in my room, at nothing in particular. It helped me to think. Even though I felt happy, the anger about my dad still felt like a long spike wedged in my heart and I wasn't sure that would ever go away. "If I forgive him," I said, "that means what he did was okay, and it wasn't okay. It wasn't even the tiniest, weeniest bit okay."

"You might never know the real reason he left. But instead of hating him, you could accept that what he did sucked, it hurt you, and it was very uncool. And then you can let it go and get on with your life."

I lay there for ages, thinking. About my dad. About my mum and them being together. About them having me and Bella, and looking so happy in those photos of when they came home from hospital with us. We were tiny and cute and helpless. How could he walk away from that and never even call?

At last, I said, "I don't think I can ever forgive him. I don't know how to. And I don't know if I want to. He might never come back and then I'll go through my whole life without a dad. You know how much that sucks?"

You nodded and let out a long slow whistle. "I know

how much that sucks. Humans make mistakes. They get angry, they do stupid things they're not proud of, and they hurt the people they love most."

It was true. I got angry and said things to Mum and to Bella that I didn't mean, and sometimes I hurt them just because I felt like it. And I always regretted it but by then it was too late.

I stared at the ceiling, thinking about what you said. Wishing I lived on the top floor and the roof was made of glass so I could see the sky. I must have eventually fallen asleep because the next thing I knew, my alarm went off and it was Sunday morning.

ThiRtY-TWO-
TRentadue-San JŪ NI

The first thing I did was groan. It was the day of Bella's party.

I got out of bed, washed my face, scrubbed my hands, and went into the kitchen.

Nonna was there, baking Bella's birthday cake. It was this great big Italian thing with cream and layers. I put on rubber gloves and washed up the cake bowl to help out. Mum was vacuuming the floor, which was pointless if you ask me when loads of kids were about to come and wreck the place. Bella was running around, totally hyperactive, "getting ready"—even though she wasn't really doing much except being in the way.

And then the phone rang.

Mum answered in a jolly voice. Then I heard her voice turn cold. She said, "What? No! Don't tell me that. Please tell me you're not serious!"

I flicked soapy water off the rubber gloves and walked toward her. "Mum? Mum, what is it?"

"NOOOOOOOO!" she screamed through the phone.

Awful things ran through my mind. Someone had died. The entire Pyke family were on their way over with weapons. We'd been kicked out of our house and we had to live under a bridge for the rest of our lives.

She put the phone down and stared hard into the space in front of her eyes with her hands over her mouth.

"Mum, what? You're scaring me. Is someone dead?"

She shook her head.

"Have we lost all our savings?"

"*Savings?* HAHAHAHAHAHA! You poor deluded child! We don't *have* any savings!"

"So who was that?"

"Clopsie the Clown. She canceled! She's sick!" Mum looked at me in horror. "What are we going to do?" Her face wasn't as white as a fridge but it was pretty white for a face.

I sighed with relief. I thought it was a miracle, a blessing, and a gift from God, but Mum didn't think so. She spent the rest of the morning on the phone but it was too late. No other entertainers were free.

"It can't be that hard to keep them occupied, can it?" Mum wailed, her fingers rapping nervously on the phone. "We'll play some party games, then they'll eat, and that'll be that. It'll be fine."

Nonna shouted, "HAH!" from the kitchen.

Mum and I looked at each other and gulped.

"Mum," I whispered, "there's still time to escape. We can get in the car and be in Paris by evening."

"Can't," Mum groaned. "Engine problems. The car's going into the garage tomorrow."

We had no choice. The party was going ahead. As the cake was baking, Nonna started making about a million sandwiches. Mum was opening bags of chips and putting sweets, grapes, and cookies on the table. I tried to help but I was a fidgety, jittery wreck. I dropped a carton of juice, tripped over a plastic bag, and knocked things off the table until Mum held me by the shoulders and said, "No one will go in your room, Amber. Any mess can be cleaned up. It's going to be fine."

"Okay. If you say so."

"Now listen to me," Mum said, "your main jobs are opening the door and watching Bella to make sure she doesn't rip open her presents as soon as they give them to her. But for now you can put out the plates and cups."

"Okay."

Once I'd finished, I closed my bedroom door, praying that none of Bella's friends would go in and destroy my belongings with their revolting, sticky, germy hands. Then I went to help Mum with the last-minute jobs.

I moved furniture and stuck banners up and put some balloons downstairs so Bella's friends would be able to find the building easily. If you think about it, balloons are pretty disgusting because they're full of germy lung air, mouth bacteria, and spit. But I tried not to think about it.

When the phone rang again, Mum ran to it. She was certain it was Clopsie calling to say she was fine but it was just one of Bella's friends phoning to say

233

she couldn't come because she was sick too. Then another one called. Then another one.

We thought it was a good time to tell Bella about Clopsie.

"Bella, there's a *terrible* bug going around!" Mum said, acting so well she should have got an award. "Grace has got it, Ben's got it, Frankie's got it and ..." Mum looked away, "the *worst* thing is, Clopsie the Clown's got it."

Bella looked at Mum, her eyes as big as beach balls. "What? Isn't Clopsie coming, Mummy?"

"Well, she can't, Bella. She's so ill with this terrible, terrible virus."

It didn't go down very well. Bella started crying and stomping her feet and yelling like a big baby until Mum pulled out the costume Nonna had bought her, still in its bag. I looked at it, confused.

"Bella," Mum said, "look at this fabulous costume Nonna bought you."

Bella stopped crying and looked at the costume. Then she wrinkled up her nose and squinted at it. "But that's not a unicorn costume," she said. "That's a police costume!"

"*Si, amore,*" Nonna said. "I told you. I buy so nice ooniform costume. You like it?"

Bella tilted her head to one side. "Ooniform?" she said, looking at the costume. Under the plastic cover was a luminous green jacket saying POLICE across the front, a hat with a black-and-white checked band, a pair of black trousers, and—dangling off the hanger—a walkie-talkie.

I looked at Nonna and laughed. "Bella thought you said it was a uni*corn* costume!"

"Ambra," Nonna said, as if I was *molto pazza* (crazy). "Me? I buy her *unicorn* costume? Pffff."

Luckily Bella thought it was funny and wanted to put it on straight away. She almost forgot about Clopsie.

"You have to make sure everyone stays near me and wants to talk to me. And ONLY me," Bella said, fixing the hat on her head.

"I'll make sure of it."

"Let me win all the games, okay?"

"Come on, Bella, I can't do that. But some of them, yes."

"And tell me the second that Dad comes."

235

"Bella—" I started to say as she struggled into the neon-green jacket with the band of black-and-white squares. *Seriously? She still thought he was coming? I was sure she'd got it by now!*

"Amber Miyamoto," she said, standing stiffly, "don't argue with me. You have to be a good girl or I will put you in jail for the rest of your life."

"The rest of my LIFE? Isn't that a bit harsh?"

She bent over the table, wrote something on a small piece of paper, and snapped it in front of my face.

I looked at the paper. It said: "*20 pownds.*"

"What's this?" I asked.

"It's a fine."

"What for? I didn't do anything!"

"For not wearing a costume to my party."

"I *am* wearing a costume. I'm dressed as a big sister."

She bent down to the coffee table and wrote something else. I was hoping it would be a ticket to let me off my fine.

I looked at the paper. "*And 25 pownds for rubish jowkes.*"

Okay, I thought. *Two can play at that game.*

236

I grabbed a piece of paper and wrote one too. I handed it to her: *"£20 for bad spelling."*

"But Amber," she said, looking up. "You can't give fines. You're not a policewoman."

As we waited for Bella's friends in our empty-looking flat, Bella found lots of things to fine me for. I couldn't wait for her friends to arrive so she would stop being a policewoman because she was the bossiest one you've ever met. I could just see her becoming one for real when she was older. And I just knew she was going to wear it to feed the ducks.

And then, at three on the dot, there was a knock at the door.

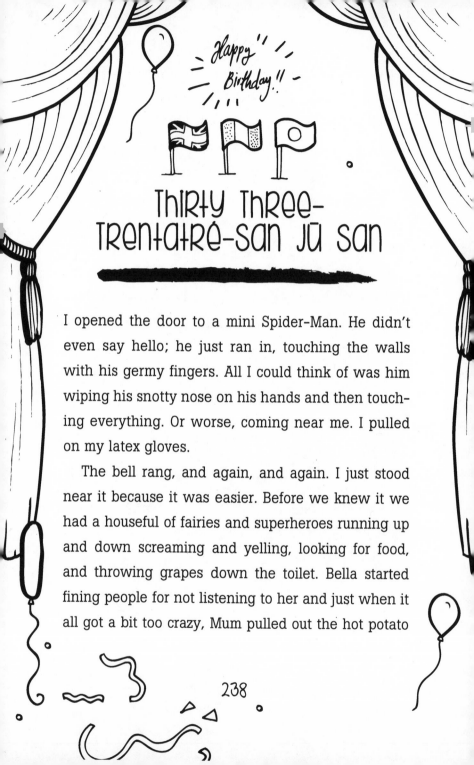

Thirty Three-
Trentatré-san jū san

I opened the door to a mini Spider-Man. He didn't even say hello; he just ran in, touching the walls with his germy fingers. All I could think of was him wiping his snotty nose on his hands and then touching everything. Or worse, coming near me. I pulled on my latex gloves.

The bell rang, and again, and again. I just stood near it because it was easier. Before we knew it we had a houseful of fairies and superheroes running up and down screaming and yelling, looking for food, and throwing grapes down the toilet. Bella started fining people for not listening to her and just when it all got a bit too crazy, Mum pulled out the hot potato game. You could see she was trying not to panic but she was looking seriously panicky.

It wasn't easy to get them all in the same room, never mind sitting in a circle. No one was listening to Mum, who was yelling for them all to come in and sit down, so I started to play the music anyway.

After about ten minutes, Mum said, "I think we made a really bad decision not to cancel the party." I had to agree. And we still had an hour and fifty minutes to go.

Worst of all, when Bella wasn't bossing her friends around she was looking out of the window every five minutes to see if Dad was coming. I kept trying to tell her he wasn't but she wasn't listening to a word I said.

To keep them amused, Mum made me do musical chairs and sleeping lions and the hokey pokey, but even after all of that, there was still one hour and forty-five minutes of the party left. Mum went a pale shade of green and looked like she needed some fresh air.

It was time to take action.

239

I gave everyone an antibacterial wipe, sat them down in a circle on the floor, and handed out sandwiches and chips. That shut them up for precisely three minutes. Then I put a movie on, even though Mum had decided not to watch a movie because really, how hard was it to entertain a bunch of six-year-olds?

Then I sank into a chair next to Mum.

"I'm telling you," she groaned, "never again. Never. Again. Clopsie the Clown is worth her weight in gold. We should have gone to Paris when we had the chance—we could have gone on the Eurostar train."

The movie wasn't so successful. Half of them were watching it and the other half were talking, which meant the ones watching couldn't hear and kept shouting at the others to shut up.

By then I didn't care. I just wanted it to be over.

Bella came over and hissed in my ear, "Amber. He's not here yet!"

"Oh, that's such a shame," I said. "Maybe you could stop looking for him out of the window and concentrate on your party. Here, give them sweets to keep them quiet."

Bella handed the sweets out. Then she checked the window again. Every time she looked out, her shoulders slumped. But she turned around and got bossy again in zero seconds flat.

Then something weird happened. Nonna started singing the Noah's Ark song loudly from the kitchen, *"Ci son due coccodrilli, ed un orangotango, due piccoli serpenti, un'aquila reale, un gatto, un topo e un elefante: non manca più nessuno; solo non si vedono i due liocorni..."*

It sounds crazy but the kids who weren't watching the DVD but instead were wandering around the house poking their hands into ornaments, opening cupboards, and hiding in wardrobes, went to sit with her.

She carried on singing and once she had them in there, she taught them *"Se sei felice e tu lo sai batti le mani"* (if you're happy and you know it clap your hands) and got them all clapping their hands and basically saved the day because she's Nonna and everyone loves her.

"Bella," I said, "let's do the cake now."

"No, Amber—wait. Dad's not here yet!" she whispered in her not-quiet-at-all voice.

What was she thinking? I mean, really.

As if my dad was going to turn up. Even if he had got the letters who knows if he'd have bothered.

"Can't wait, Bella. We have to do it now or not at all."

I knew that would work.

I paused the movie and Nonna brought the cake. All Bella's noisy, messy little friends sang "Happy Birthday" to her. We even lifted her up on a chair, which she was so pleased about, she took back one of my fines. Then she made a wish and cut the first slice.

While Mum put the movie back on, Nonna and I took the cake to the table, cut it into pieces, and I wrapped each piece about six times in plastic wrap so they couldn't open it in the house. Mum came in and started eating all the leftover sandwiches. She had a glazed look in her eyes. "These have been the longest two hours of my life," she said, "and they're not over yet."

When the movie ended, we fed them more sweets. At exactly the point when the sugar rush

was kicking in, their parents started arriving to collect them. The kids went out with their wrapped-up cake and their party favors. Bella started moaning that she wanted to do it again next week but with Clopsie this time.

As if.

Soon there were only two children left in the house apart from Bella. Mum was stuffing wrapping paper from the pass the parcel into a black trash bag, so I answered the door when it rang.

Locker Boy was standing there, smiling.

I froze.

"Hi. I'm here to pick up my brother, Miguel," he said. "Sorry I'm late."

"Oh. Right." I turned into a wooden pole. Rigid and straight and silent.

"I saw you won the art competition."

I nodded like a brainless, tongueless moron.

"Your drawing is totally awesome."

I felt my cheeks burn bright red. "Oh…thanks."

"And," he said, grinning and looking at his feet, "Amber Miyamoto is, like, the coolest name ever. It

sounds like a cartoon character of a samurai girl or a ninja spy or something."

I laughed. "Actually, my name's Ambra. My mum's Italian."

"Ammmbrrra," he said, saying it the right way, with a roly-poly "r" and a chewy "m." I was so shocked.

And then he said, "Can I ask you something?"

Gulp. He was going to ask me what the other half was and once he heard it, he would think I was really weird and alien. Or maybe he'd think I was unique and special and would ask me all about Japan. Not that I knew anything.

"Sure."

"Why are you wearing plastic gloves?"

"Oh."

I glanced down at my hands. I couldn't exactly tell him the truth: that I was obsessively worried about dirt. That I hated germs. That birthday parties for six-year-olds were full of potential hazards.

I think it was then that I decided, *Enough, Amber. You have to get over this. This is too crazy.*

"Umm, I have a bit of a problem...but I'm hoping it'll go away soon."

"Yeah, I think my cousin has that too. Eczema, right? Her skin is so red and dry that she can't touch water and has to wear gloves."

"Ambra, *perché non gli hai chiesto di entrare*? Why you no ask de nice boy inside?" said Nonna, arriving at the door.

"Oh. Sorry! I'm such an idiot. Come in."

He laughed. "Thanks. My dad's waiting in the car so I can't stay long."

He came in and stood in the hallway as Nonna walked away, chuckling.

I turned around and yelled, "Miguel! Your brother's here!"

"By the way, my name's Luis," he said.

AS IF I DIDN'T KNOW!

"I did tell you once but you probably don't remember. Luis Fernandez."

"Where's your name from? Is it Spanish or something?"

"My dad's from Mexico and my mum's Scottish. I'm a weird mix."

I grinned and nodded. "Yeah, I know that one."

We stood there feeling the most uncomfortable

anyone has ever felt in the history of the world (probably) until I said, "Can I ask *you* something?"

"Sure."

"Do you draw?"

He made a face. "Kind of. Not really."

"But—how come you had a portfolio in school?"

"I brought some of my photos in to show the art teacher."

"You're a *photographer*?"

He shrugged. "I take photos. I wouldn't exactly say I was a photographer."

"Oh. Wow. Did you enter the school competition?"

"No. I do these photos but then add drawings over the top of them. I play around with them so it's not straight photography. I'm still learning. It's not like your stuff or anything."

Not like my stuff? Like I was some kind of proper artist? My cheeks went scarlet.

"I'd really like to learn more about drawing though—to play with my photographs more. Do you think you could show me how you do some of your artwork?" he asked. "Oh…no, I shouldn't have asked. You're probably busy. Forget it."

"Course I can show you."

His brown eyes widened to huge circles. "Really?"

"No problem."

He smiled a smile like a massive firework exploding in the center of the universe, causing the biggest spray of light that whizzed to the farthest parts and went on shining forever. My stomach did an Olympic gold-medal-winning triple backflip.

And then Miguel arrived and ran out of the door over my feet, crushing my small toe.

"Your gloves look dumb," he said.

"Sorry about my brother. He's a bit of a handful."

"Oh, he's okay," I said. I'm such a good liar. The only reason I would ever, ever let that revolting boy in my house again was because of his big brother.

Luis turned to leave.

"Do you want to meet me at lunchtime tomorrow in the art room?" I said.

Luis turned back and smiled, as his stupid squirt of a brother ran to their car.

"I mean, art club is every Wednesday after school," I went on, "but they go to the art room most lunchtimes as well. I'm sure it's okay if you come along. And maybe bring your portfolio—I'd love to see your photos."

"*¡Fenómeno!*" he said.

Which I guessed was "great" in Spanish. Or maybe Scottish.

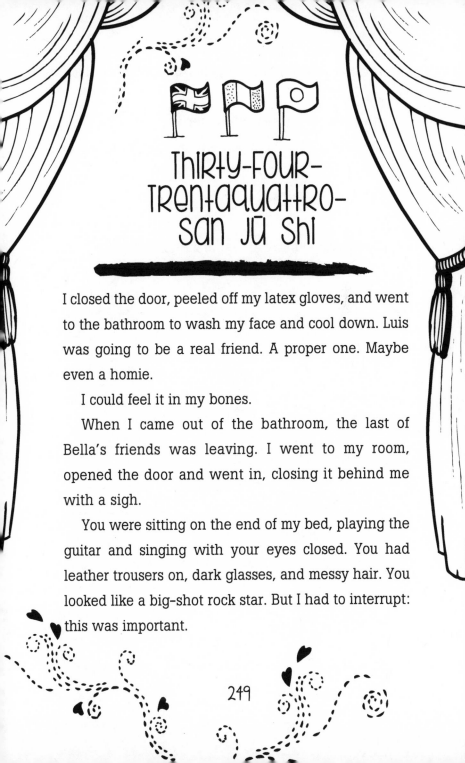

Thirty-four-
Trentaquattro-
san jū shi

I closed the door, peeled off my latex gloves, and went to the bathroom to wash my face and cool down. Luis was going to be a real friend. A proper one. Maybe even a homie.

I could feel it in my bones.

When I came out of the bathroom, the last of Bella's friends was leaving. I went to my room, opened the door and went in, closing it behind me with a sigh.

You were sitting on the end of my bed, playing the guitar and singing with your eyes closed. You had leather trousers on, dark glasses, and messy hair. You looked like a big-shot rock star. But I had to interrupt: this was important.

"He was here! Picking up his brother! He talked to me!"

You opened your eyes but carried on strumming. "Oh yeah? Did he punch you on the arm? Make fun of you? Throw things at you or call you names?"

"Err…no. But he smiled."

"Yay!"

"And guess what? He wants me to show him how to draw."

"Yeah, yeah, that's just one of those tricks boys use, you know, to get to know you better."

"Maybe. But I don't think so."

"Hah! You've got a lot to learn. I watched a whole show about it on *Life On Planet Boy*. Did you survive the party?"

"Just about. I have to go and help Mum clear up now. There's still time for a bacterial and toxic disaster to be discovered."

"Right."

I came over and stood right in front of you.

You stopped strumming and looked up at me.

"What?"

"What do I do about Bella?"

"You have to tell her it was you. You know that."

"I can't do it."

"Yeah, you can. It's the right thing. You have to 'fess up."

I sighed and slumped on to the bed beside you.

"She's going to be so upset about it."

"You can do it, Amber."

I breathed out long and hard. And then went out to face the music.

"Oh, there you are. Come and help me clear up," Mum said.

I put my gloves on again, but clearing up was easy. There was no cat litter, which always helps. And there were no major disasters, like giant slimy boogers on the chairs or chocolate handprints on the walls. I wiped everything with antibacterial wipes as Mum vacuumed the floor again. I knew it was pointless to do it before the party. Nonna was putting a gazillion leftover sandwiches in plastic wrap and in the fridge, and Bella was licking the icing off half of the leftover cupcakes so no one else would ever want to eat them.

Gross.

"Can I open my presents now?" Bella asked, staring at the large pile with her huge eyes shining.

"Of course," Mum said. "As long as you stop giving me fines."

We all went to sit with Bella as she went through her pile of presents. Mum got a pen and paper. She likes to write down who sent us what so she can bribe us to write thank-you cards.

Nonna was so excited you'd have thought it was her birthday and her mountain of presents. She made it such fun for Bella, clapping her hands and screeching, "Oh my goodness, juss look how many presents you get! You such a lucky girl! Muss be a hundred presents here!"

I loved my nonna so much for that. More than usual even, and I usually love her loads.

I watched Bella open one after another of the pink, plastic, glittery, useless presents from her friends, but then she saw a large one wrapped in gold paper.

"Ooh, this one's big!" Bella read out the tag. "It says, "To Bella. I love you very much"."

"Is that it?" Mum asked. "No name to say who it's from?"

"No."

"Oh. That's strange."

Bella ripped open the wrapping.

When she saw what was inside she screamed, punched the air with both arms and shouted, "YESSSSS! LOOK! Look what I got! Look!"

It was a Sparkle Girl Jewelry Maker, and on top of it, taped on, was a purple Swatch watch.

Bella held up the box and danced around the room, screeching.

"I don't understand it," Mum said, looking at Nonna and me. "Who bought her those? They're expensive presents—they're not from her friends. And who would say they love her very much?"

"Someone who loves me and will always look after me," Bella said.

And I grinned because it was true.

"Amber?" Mum said, her eyes whipping toward me. "AMBER, YOU DIDN'T!"

I looked at her and smiled. She gasped so loudly

I thought she'd seen a giant tarantula creeping up behind me with its jaws open.

"You spent all your hard-earned money on Bella's birthday presents?! I thought you were saving for a phone! I can't believe you did that!"

Mum had tears in her eyes and she started flapping at her face like she was hot.

"No, Mum," Bella said, looking shocked, "this isn't from Amber. This is from someone else."

"Bella," I said, tugging her sleeve, "I think we should go into your room for a minute. I have to talk to you."

As we went out, I heard Mum saying to Nonna, "I can't believe she did that. Can you believe she did that?"

When we got into Bella's room I shut the door.

"They're from HIM!" Bella squealed. "They're from Dad! They're exactly what I asked him for!"

"Bella, they're not. I have to tell you something."

I stood in front of her. She looked at me with hopeful eyes.

I gulped.

This was the hardest thing I'd ever had to do. I felt so terrible the words just got stuck in my chest.

254

"Wait!" Bella said. She ran to her pillow and put her hand under it.

"Bella, seriously. This is important," I said.

She pulled out an envelope and handed it to me. It was another letter. She hadn't even written the name on the front yet.

"Oh no," I groaned. "Bella, I have to tell you something," I said.

"What? You're not really my sister?"

"No, I'm definitely your sister. Can you please shush and let me say it? It's really hard and you're not making it easy for me."

"Okay, but I have to do a wee-wee first or I'll do it on the floor," she said, and she ran out.

Ew.

When she was out, I sighed. I was so scared of telling her the truth. She would stand there in her policewoman's outfit, looking crushed. A huge fat tear would roll out of her eye, just like when we stood watching that girl and her dad in the sandpit, and we'd be right back at stage one.

And then I got worried.

I'd be in serious trouble if Mum found out.

I'd have to threaten to take all those presents back to the shop so Bella wouldn't tell on me.

Bella was taking ages. I noticed the envelope wasn't even sealed so I ran behind her door and slid the letter out, hoping she wouldn't catch me.

It said:

Dier Amber,

Thank you for writting letters to me and preetendin to be Daddy. It was reli fun writtin letters wiht yu. I liket the big secrut. I wish Dad was hear but I'm very happy you are my big sister.

Love, Bella

PS Im macking you a lovly pink and yelow braslet with hearts and flowas that you have to wear allways, even in the showah and in karate.

She'd worked it out. The crafty little—

I knocked on the bathroom door.

"What?" she shouted.

"You knew?"

She started laughing the laugh of an evil ruler who wants to take over the world.

As I sat outside the bathroom waiting for her to come out, I tried to work out when she knew. Maybe it was right at the beginning, with the very first letter. Or, more likely, just at the end, when I wrote the last one.

When she came out of the bathroom, she was grinning.

"You're not angry with me?" I asked.

"Only this much," she said. She was showing about an inch between her fingers. Then she gave me a big hug. I wanted to let her do it but she'd just been to the toilet and you could bet your life she hadn't scrubbed her hands. So I unhooked her arms and said, "Bella, you have to promise me you won't tell Mum about the letters because she'll freak out."

"Okay."

"No, really, Bella. If you tell Mum, I'm taking that jewelry maker back to the shop."

"No!"

"Yes! AND the Swatch watch."

"No, Amber, please!"

"So don't tell her."

"Okay, okay."

"I'm serious, Bella. Whenever I tell you not to tell Mum, you always do. This time you have to promise me or those go back straight away. Look at me. Promise."

She wiped her snotty nose on her sleeve, which was *ew*. "I promise."

"No, but do you promisey promise with the extra promisey bit?"

She sniffed. "Really, Amber," she said, "sometimes you're so babyish."

Then she turned around, ran into the sitting room, and continued trying to break the impossible-to-open plastic shields off her presents. I have no idea why they make toys childproof.

Mum and Nonna were talking quietly together.

When I walked in Mum said, "Amber, can we have a word with you?"

"Sure."

I sat down, seriously hoping she hadn't overheard our little conversation. I picked some icing off an unlicked cupcake, even though it was pink. *Mmm.*

"Amber, we're so touched that you spent all your money on Bella. We just can't believe you'd do something so considerate and thoughtful when all this time we were sure you were saving for a phone."

I squirmed in my seat. I didn't deserve this honor. Mainly because I would much rather have bought a phone.

"Well…you don't know the whole story…" I said, my tongue zinging from the sugar.

"Maybe not, but we've agreed that as a reward for winning the art competition and because you did something so generous and kind, Nonna and I are going to buy you a new phone."

"WHAT??"

"Tomorrow, right after school."

Nonna pulled me over to her and slammed me down on to her large lap.

259

"You diss-erve it, *amore*," she said, and hugged me so hard, the air whooshed out of my lungs.

After Nonna left, I went into my room, put my school-bag on the floor and sighed a big, contented sigh.

You were sitting at my desk with your guitar by your side. It was in its case and you were dressed in jeans, a hoodie, running shoes, and a baseball cap. You looked quite normal. For you.

"Hey," I said.

You turned to me and smiled. "Hey yourself. Everything okay?"

"Yeah. Everything's great, actually. It's all worked out really well."

"Very glad to hear it. Got some friends now?"

"Yep. I even have some homies."

You chuckled and tugged the brim of your cap. "All sorted with Bella?"

"Yep. All sorted."

"What about that black hole of yours. Has it gone?"

"Nah. Not exactly. It still swirls around in there, all dark and heavy and stuff. But at least I killed the beast, right?"

"You sure did. That was audacious. Talking of which, how's the fearless warrior coming on—did you find Ninja Amber buried deep inside you somewhere?"

"No, but I think I know where she's hiding. I can't be sure she's there because I didn't get around to kicking Joanne Pyke's butt but I didn't need to in the end."

You grinned and stood up. "Nearly covered everything, then, didn't we? Wait—you wanted to feel whole. Not half this and half that. How's that going?"

I thought about it for a second. "I'm still half this and half that," I said, "and I always will be. My dad's not around and I still don't know anyone in the whole world who's Japanese, so there's this entire half missing. But I feel a bit better about that now. I've got my mum and Nonna and Bella, and the truth is, we're a family without him. Plus, I'm not the only one who's a salad."

"Too right. You just keep remembering that," you said. "There are loads of awesome salads walking around all over the place. I'm proud of you, Amber. So listen up. I'm going away now."

I looked at you in surprise. "Oh, you are?" Then I

noticed it. There was a suitcase at the end of my bed. And you did seem sort of ready to go somewhere. I hadn't really realized it until then.

"I am. But you'll be fine. I have this hunch."

I nodded. It was strange. I didn't feel sad or anything that you were leaving. Inventing you was possibly the best thing that had ever happened to me. It was amazing. It had changed my life. But I had a funny feeling I was going to be okay. For a while, anyway. But what if I needed you again?

"Sooo...are you coming back?"

"That's entirely up to you," you said, picking up your suitcase and your guitar. "If you ever need me, I'll be right here. Any time at all. Just give me a shout."

And *paff*.

You were gone.

Acknowledgements

This book would not be in your hands if it were not for a serendipitous meeting with Barry Cunningham, so first and foremost, thank you, Barry. A huge thank you to Rachel H, Tina, Laura, Elinor, and all at Chicken House for all their hard work and good humor, and a Japanese-style bow of gratitude and respect to Rachel Leyshon, (probably) the most insightful, good-natured, and diplomatic editor the world has ever known. Thank you too to Allison Hellegers at The Rights People, and to Aubrey Poole and the outstanding team at Sourcebooks for taking Amber across the pond and giving her a great look and a happy home in the U.S. and Canada.

Thank you to Ariko(-san) Nishimura for help with the Japanese numbers, and to Amber, Luna, Marina, Marco, and Susie who helped with the Italian. Thanks to Helen Crawford-White, and to Sean Gaston and David Fulton at Brunel University for their encouragement and support

Toda raba to Asi and the Shevach family, and

love to Aunty Eileen, may her memory be blessed, for being amazing when I needed it. T'anks a million to my extended clans (Irish, Italian, Thai, Israeli, American) and to my most excellent colleagues and friends for supporting me, enriching my life, and keeping me smiling.

I'm honoured to have Tamar, Maor, Maayan and Natan in my life. You guys are the greatest gift of all, better than anything, and I'm blessed to spend every single day with you, watching you grow into the most amazing people on the planet.

And lastly, I know there are uncountable excellent fathers, and many who want to see their children but can't, and I have only respect and admiration for you. But this last word of thanks goes to mothers everywhere who, despite the hurdles and the tiredness, despite being undercompensated and undervalued, do their best every single day for their children, especially my own remarkable mother. I thank you for your love and your strength, and for bringing us up alone with no one to help you. No one to share the bills with you or fix the taps when they broke. No one to help you decide whether we were really too ill to

265

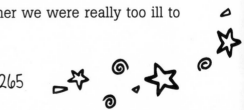

go to school that day or if we were just pretending. You had to make every decision on your own. You worked hard every day and you had to be everything to us. And you still are.

Dara Palmer's Major Drama

Dara Palmer knows she's destined to be a
star. The problem is, the rest of the world
hasn't seemed to figure that out yet…

1

I never thought I'd say this, but nuns and noodles can change your life. Well, maybe they don't change **everyone's**, but they definitely changed mine. And not just once either, which is so freaky I don't even know how to measure it with a spoon.

No one thinks nuns are going to be life-changing. Sorry, but that's the truth. Especially not the kind of nuns who sing in trees and make clothes out of curtains like Maria in *The Sound of Music*, which is a musical extravaganza about not-your-usual-type-of-nun and whistling captains and singing children and double-crossing Nazi boyfriends and female deer and lonely goatherds high on a hill singing "layohlayohlay-eeh-oh." Which sounds nuts, I know, but it kind of makes sense when you see the movie. Kind of. It's still pretty nuts though, even then.

And I don't even like noodles. But if something's going to change your life, I guess noodles are better than the Black Death, a monster earthquake, a plague of poisonous frogs, or a million other terrible things.

This all happened a while ago now. Let me just say, I was a different person back then. I don't know if you're going to like the old me much when you hear what I was like, but I've changed. Stuff happened along the way— all kinds of stuff, actually. Nuns and noodles were just the beginning.

So maybe we should start there. At the very beginning. It's a very good place to start.

NOODLES! VS. BLACK DEATH

2

It was a Wednesday morning in March, which is normally not even remotely exciting, but this one was special. We had less than two weeks left of school before spring break, which meant our music and drama teacher, Miss Snarling, was going to hold auditions for the end-of-the-year play **any day** now. She always held them at the end of the spring quarter so everyone knew their parts before spring break.

Lacey and I were mega-hyped about the play. That morning, we went into school bursting like exploding watermelons because the auditions had to be in the next few days. You have to understand, Lacey and I were **desperate** to star in it. And I mean STAR. As in lead role. As in big deal. As in loads of lines and even more attention. As in bouquets of flowers and standing

ovations. As in give-me-that-part-or-I-will-die-right-here-on-the-floor.

We'd never had lead roles before. We'd never had any decent parts at all, for some mysterious reason, but this year it was different. We were in fifth grade now, and fifth graders always got the biggest parts because they were leaving for middle school. This year, our lives were going to change upside-down-edly and it was all going to start with the end-of-the-year play.

We got in trouble for chatting, for fidgeting, and then for not listening, and that was only in the first ten minutes of class. Even after Mr. Foxx sent us to sit on the quiet table for ten minutes, we were still like wind-up toys when you've just wound them up. I sat there dreaming of driving around Hollywood in my red convertible car with everyone taking photos of me. I don't know what Lacey was dreaming of, but you could bet your bottom on your dollar that her dreams were just like mine.

Lacey-Lou Davis loved drama as much as I did, which was why she was my best friend for ever and ever (BFFEAE). We were both going to be actors when we grew up. We were going to leave dry, boring England and move to America, where all the houses

are mansions, all the taxis are yellow, and everyone's rich and beautiful. Lacey was moving to LA and I was moving to Hollywood. We were going to be global megastars but stay BFFEAE and eat lunch together in fancy restaurants. We had it all planned.

I was great at acting. Even Lacey said so, and Lacey knew everything about acting. She'd have told you right away if you were terrible. She told the others in our class all the time, which didn't make her massively popular. In fact, my other friends hassled me for hanging out with her, but what could I do? She was my BFFEAE. We were going places.

When Mr. Foxx called us back to our usual tables, our heads were full of *buzshuzziness*. We couldn't focus on our schoolwork even if we wanted to, and we really didn't want to because, let's face it, school in real life is sleeve-chewingly boring. School in the movies is way more fun. No one ever does any work; they just hang around the lockers talking to boys with flicky hair, bicker with nasty rich girls, and then jump in their cars and drive to the mall.

I love movies. I think about them every hour of every day and I act out movies in my head, like, all the time. I especially

love Bradley Porter (best actor ever) and Liberty Lee (best actress ever. Actually, you're supposed to call everyone an actor now, even women, which I know about because show business is my life). I watch everything they're in over and over again, even though half the time I have no idea what they're talking about. There's this whole language I don't understand, with words like proms and pageants and homecoming and vanity cases and tenth grade and Thanksgiving. I'm, like, Huh? What are all those things?

Even though I was good at acting, I still practiced so I could get as good as Liberty Lee. Every night I made faces in front of the mirror, like being surprised and sad and delighted. My best face was the one where someone says a stinging comment and you look to the side and think long and hard about it (which you have to do in soap operas).

Lacey even agreed that that was my best face. Her best face is shock. She's so good at it! I just know she'll get parts in movies where she's, like, in the sea all relaxed and she looks up and there's a massive tidal wave coming (close-up of her face) and she freaks out, turns around to swim away and sees a gigantic shark right in front of her with its jaws open. There are loads of movies like that. She's going to be SO famous.

I could do surprised faces but they weren't as good as Lacey's. I could cry better than Lacey though—I'd been working on it. My secret was that I imagined an earthquake ripping up our road, making our house collapse, and my parents and my brother Felix got trapped in the rubble. They didn't die or anything; I'm not that mean. But the panic of not knowing whether they were alive or dead made me cry in zero seconds flat.

I wasn't proud to admit my technique, but it really worked. The tears welled up and came rolling out of my eyes. I'm sure that's how Liberty Lee does it as well.

After the first lesson, Mr. Foxx announced that the fifth graders had to go into the hall for an assembly. Lacey and I squealed at each other with outstretched eyes and flapped our hands in excite-a-panic.

This was it!

We scurried in and sat on the floor with our legs crossed, jiggling our knees. Miss Snarling stood up, holding a hefty pile of paper. She was wearing a yellow cardigan, black trousers, and yellow shoes so she looked a bit like a giant wasp. Her name suited her down to the ground—Lacey reckoned her first name was "Always." She was the meanest music and drama teacher ever and she always

chose the most boring old-fashioned plays no one even liked. Last year she picked *Little Shop of Horrors* and we were like...huh? Little what of what?

"Good morning, everyone," she said. She was tall and wide with a gap in her teeth and a bush of curly hair like Medusa snakes, and she always wore at least one thing that was yellow. I'm sorry but nobody wears yellow. Maybe they do in India or the Caribbean or places where it's hot and happy, but not in London. It's just...wrong.

"I'm happy to announce that we will be holding auditions today for the end-of-the-year play, which will be..."

Lacey yelped. I held my breath. *Who Stole My Brain?*, I thought. *Please say* Who Stole My Brain?

"*The Sound of Music!*"

Huh? Lacey and I looked at each other in horror. The what?

It sounded so lame.

It was ancient for sure. Everyone else looked as confused as we did.

"As some of you may not know *The Sound of Music*, I'll briefly outline the story, and Mrs. Lefkowitz has agreed to

Miss Snarling

274

let us watch the first half of it now. It's a long film so we can't see it all, but you'll have enough of an idea by then and we can watch the rest after spring break."

Oooh, yay! OK, it wasn't *Who Stole My Brain?* but watching a movie instead of having lessons almost made up for it. This was turning into a **very good day!**

Miss Snarling explained the story (weird) and then closed the curtains. My knees were jiggling so hard I had to put my hands on them to calm them down. She started the film and in a second, we *shuummmed* back in time to the olden days.

I tell you, *The Sound of Music* might have been ancient but it was **so good**. When she turned the film off, everyone went, "Ooooowwwwwhhhh" even though it was recess, which everyone knows is the best part of school.

Miss Snarling clapped her hands and said, "The auditions will be in here after recess. Those of you who don't want to be in the play, please stay in your classrooms with your teachers."

I already knew who I wanted to be. More than anything ever in my entire life, I wanted to be Maria. I wanted to be her so much my bones ached, my head hurt, and

my blood went *zizzy*. I knew I'd be perfect. Better than Lacey. I mean, Lacey had the right face: she had sticky-toffee hair and peanut-butter eyes and a nose like a right-angled triangle. Her hair was long and she wore it in a high pony with a braid so it looked a long rope coming off the top of her head. She had a lazy left eye and a chin dimple, but apart from that, she almost looked like Maria in the film. But Lacey sings like a cat with its head stuck in a lawnmower. I was hoping she could be Liesl though, and then we'd both have main parts.

"I mean it, Lacey," I murmured as we stood up to leave, "if we don't get lead roles this year, I'll—"

"I know!" Lacey hooted. "If we don't, I'm writing to the Prime Minister and the Queen. I so will as well. I don't even care—"

"Um, girls!" Mr. Foxx snapped, making us jump sky high. "You two chatterboxes don't have to blurt out every single thought that comes into your heads, you know."

Lacey and I looked at each other and were like, umm. Course we do. Duh.

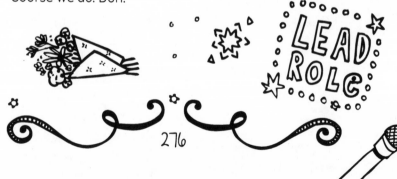

LEAD ROLE

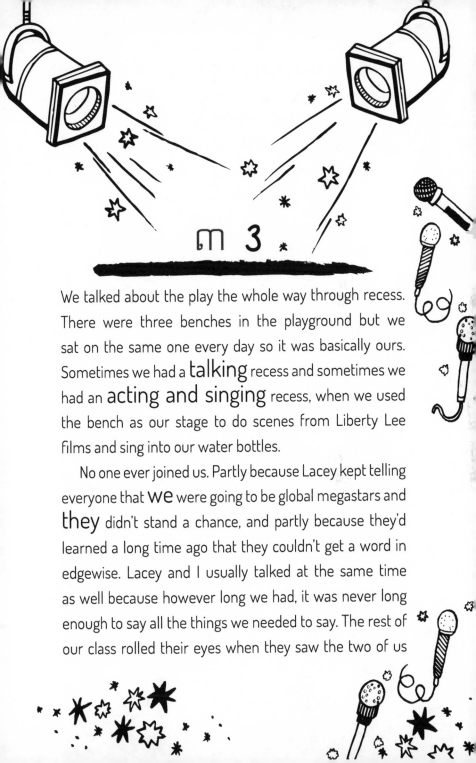

3

We talked about the play the whole way through recess. There were three benches in the playground but we sat on the same one every day so it was basically ours. Sometimes we had a **talking** recess and sometimes we had an **acting and singing** recess, when we used the bench as our stage to do scenes from Liberty Lee films and sing into our water bottles.

No one ever joined us. Partly because Lacey kept telling everyone that **we** were going to be global megastars and **they** didn't stand a chance, and partly because they'd learned a long time ago that they couldn't get a word in edgewise. Lacey and I usually talked at the same time as well because however long we had, it was never long enough to say all the things we needed to say. The rest of our class rolled their eyes when they saw the two of us coming, but that was something we just had to get used to. Lacey says the first thing actors need to learn is this: not everyone can deal with your talent.

After the bell rang, we still hadn't finished talking. They should definitely make recess at least an hour.

All through the next class, when we were supposed to be doing mental math, I practiced doing Maria's faces: shocked when she sees the whistles for the kids, kind-but-teacherish when they run into her room during the thunderstorm, and sappy when she gazes at Captain von Trapp. I got some funny looks from Mr. Foxx but I didn't even care.

There was just one itty-bitty problem.

Miss Snarling. She **totally hated** Lacey and me. I don't even know why. She never gave us any main parts. We'd both wanted to be Tracy in *Hairspray* and Audrey in *Little Shop of Horrors* and we were devastated when Miss Snarling gave them to Ella Moss-Daniels.

It was **SO** not fair. Ella Moss-Daniels acted like a three-legged dog in a blender. She'd had main parts even when we were little. Lacey said it was because Ella's mum was chair of the PTA and her dad gave the school a big donation for the library—nothing to do with her acting or anything. I asked my dad if he would give a big donation to the library too, but he just looked at me in a way that said rude things without actually saying anything rude with his mouth. Dad was good at that look. I was going to have to try it.

I was a teaspoonful of worried. If I didn't get the part of Maria, I was probably going to curl up in a ball and die. It was that bad.

"NEXT!"

At the auditions, I went up fourteenth. The thirteen people before me were as lame as a one-legged donkey with a broken ankle, so I knew I stood a chance.

I had to read the part where Maria arrives at the von Trapp house to meet the children. Then I had to sing the song. You know, the song. The one with raindrops and roses and kittens with mittens and brown paper packages tied up with strings (which, by the way, I've never even seen, so it wouldn't be one of my favorite things).

Anyway, I rocked. It was the best audition I'd ever done. The whole way through, Miss Snarling's face looked like a lizard dying on a rock, but I ignored her. I also ignored Ella Moss-Daniels, Abi Compton, Kezia Krantz, Benji Hyer, and all the others in the hall who were rolling their eyes and smirking, because what did they know? They couldn't even act, which is why they had to go to Miss Snarling's drama classes. Lacey and I were way beyond that.

I knew I'd done well. You can just feel these things in your lower intestines. Lacey's audition was great too. I was a teaspoonful of worried that she'd get Maria instead of me, but it was never going to happen. Lacey can act, sure, but she can't sing to save her life. I'd never tell her that, obviously. Some things you can't even tell your best friend if you still want her to be your best friend afterward.

While the others auditioned, Lacey and I sat in the back. We couldn't stop talking about the different parts and who should be which of the minor characters—we had it all worked out. All Miss Snarling had to do was ask and we'd have told her how to cast the whole thing.

Bubbles of excitement fizzled through us from top to toe. We were like bottles of pop that fell out of the fridge and went *dung-duh-dung-duh-dung* on the floor.

That afternoon, we were called back into the hall.
Miss Snarling was announcing the results.

THE SOUND OF MUSIC

About the Author

My name is Emma Shevah, and I was born and raised in London. My mother is Irish and my father was Thai, and I'm proud to tell you, I can actually say and write both those sentences in Thai. I can't say much more than that yet, though—I'm still learning.

I studied English Literature and Philosophy at Nottingham University and when I graduated, I worked for a while and then went traveling for years and years. I did some weird jobs (like fire juggling, jewelry selling, and ear piercing) and lived for a while in Australia, Japan, India (where our first child was born in the Himalayas) and Jerusalem (I know how to say and write all this in Hebrew too) before moving back to the UK with my family and doing a Masters in Creative and Professional Writing at Brunel. I like nothing better than flying away on an adventure, although having four children, a depressed tortoise, and a constantly escaping dog makes far flung travel a little more difficult than I would like it to be.